The
Elephant's Tale

LEGEND OF THE
ANIMAL HEALER

The
Elephant's Tale

LAUREN ST. JOHN

Dial Books for Young Readers
an imprint of Penguin Group (USA) Inc.

Walden Media

DIAL BOOKS FOR YOUNG READERS
A division of Penguin Young Readers Group
Published by The Penguin Group
Penguin Group (USA) Inc., 375 Hudson Street, New York, NY 10014, U.S.A.

Penguin Group (Canada), 90 Eglinton Avenue East, Suite 700, Toronto, Ontario, Canada M4P 2Y3 (a division of Pearson Penguin Canada Inc.) • Penguin Books Ltd, 80 Strand, London WC2R 0RL, England • Penguin Ireland, 25 St. Stephen's Green, Dublin 2, Ireland (a division of Penguin Books Ltd) • Penguin Group (Australia), 250 Camberwell Road, Camberwell, Victoria 3124, Australia (a division of Pearson Australia Group Pty Ltd) • Penguin Books India Pvt Ltd, 11 Community Centre, Panchsheel Park, New Delhi - 110 017, India • Penguin Group (NZ), 67 Apollo Drive, Rosedale, North Shore 0632, New Zealand (a division of Pearson New Zealand Ltd) • Penguin Books (South Africa) (Pty) Ltd, 24 Sturdee Avenue, Rosebank, Johannesburg 2196, South Africa • Penguin Books Ltd, Registered Offices: 80 Strand, London WC2R 0RL, England

This book is published in partnership with Walden Media, LLC. Walden Media and the Walden Media skipping stone logo are trademarks and registered trademarks of Walden Media, LLC, 17 New England Executive Park, Building 17, Suite 305, Burlington MA 01803

First published in the United States 2010 by Dial Books for Young Readers
Published in Great Britain 2009 by Orion Children's Books
Copyright © 2009 by Lauren St. John

Designed by Nancy R. Leo-Kelly • Text set in Miller Text
Printed in the U.S.A.
1 3 5 7 9 10 8 6 4 2

Library of Congress Cataloging-in-Publication Data
St. John, Lauren, date.
The elephant's tale / Lauren St. John.
p. cm. — (Legend of the Animal Healer)
Summary: A fourth prophecy, this time involving elephants, comes true for eleven-year-old Martine, an orphaned South African girl with mystical healing powers over animals, when she and her grandmother are faced with losing the Sawubona Game Reserve forever.
ISBN 978-0-8037-3291-9
[1. Elephants—Fiction. 2. Wildlife conservation—Fiction.
3. Human-animal relationships—Fiction. 4. Prophecies—Fiction.
5. Orphans—Fiction. 6. Namibia—Fiction. 7. South Africa—Fiction.] I. Title.
PZ7.S77435El 2010   [Fic]—dc22   2009009285

*For my niece, Alexandra Summer,
who, being my sister's daughter, is guaranteed to
grow up wanting to save elephants!*

1

The first time Martine saw the car, she was high up on the escarpment at Sawubona Wildlife Reserve tucking into a campfire breakfast. She didn't take much notice of it then because Tendai, the Zulu game warden, distracted her by saying something to make her laugh, and because she was too busy savoring the smoky-sweet taste of her bacon and fried banana roll, and also because the car—a black limousine with blacked-out windows— turned around before it reached the distant house and went away, so she just thought it was someone lost.

It wasn't until the following day, when the black car came again while she was tending to the sanctuary animals, that she remembered the strange, slow circuit it had made, as if it were in a funeral procession. This time she had no choice but to pay attention to it, because it glided up to the runs housing Sawubona's injured and orphaned animals as if it had a right to be there. The rear door opened and a tall bald man wearing an expensive navy suit and a watch that could have been hand-crafted from a gold ingot stepped out. He looked around as if he owned the place.

"Can I help you?" she asked, trying not to show how annoyed she was that he and his big car had frightened the sick animals. She was prepared to bet that he wouldn't dream of driving into a human hospital and disturbing the patients, but a lot of people didn't feel that animals deserved the same consideration.

"Oh, I think I've seen all I need to see," he said. But he continued to stand there, a pleased smile playing around his lips. He reached into his pocket for a lighter and a fat cigar, and began puffing away as if he had all the time in the world.

"We're not open for safaris on Sunday," Martine told him. "You'll have to make an appointment and come back during the week."

"I'm not here for a safari," said the man. "I'm here to see Gwyn Thomas. And who might you be?"

Martine smothered a sigh. She had three very hungry caracals to feed and an antelope wound to dress, and she wasn't in the mood for small talk. Added to which, her grandmother had given her all the usual speeches about not speaking to strangers, although she hadn't said anything about what to do if a stranger who'd come to Sawubona on official business started plying her with questions. "I'm Martine Allen," she said reluctantly. "If you want to see my grandmother, she's at the house."

"Allen?" he repeated. "How long have you lived here, young Martine? You don't sound South African. Where are you from?"

Martine was getting desperate. She wished Tendai or Ben, her best friend in the world apart from Jemmy, her white giraffe, would show up and rescue her, but Tendai had gone into Storm Crossing to buy supplies for the reserve, and Ben was at the Waterfront in Cape Town seeing off his mum and dad. They were leaving on a Mediterranean cruise. She wanted to tell the bald man that her name and where she came from were none of his business, but she was afraid to be rude to him in case he was an important customer.

"A year," she replied. "I've been at Sawubona for nearly a year." She could have added, *Ever since my mum and dad died in a fire at our home in Hampshire, England, last New Year's Eve,* but she didn't because she was not in the habit of sharing her private information with nosy strangers. Instead she asked, "Is my grandmother expecting you? I can show you to the house."

"A year is a good long time," remarked the man. "Long enough to become attached to the place."

Then he said something that sent chills through Martine. He said: "Shame."

Just like that. Just one word: "Shame."

He said it in a way that made Martine want to rush home and take a shower, she was so creeped out, even though he had in fact been perfectly polite and kept his distance throughout. His only crime had been polluting Sawubona's wildlife hospital with his cigar.

Before Martine could come up with a response, he

continued briskly: "Right, then, I think it's time I had a word with your grandmother. Don't trouble yourself, I know the way."

He climbed back into his shiny black car and was chauffeured away, leaving the sickly smell of cigar smoke and that one weighted word hanging in the air.

"Shame."

2

After he'd gone, Martine considered taking the shortcut to the house to warn her grandmother that a sinister man was on his way, but she hadn't thought to ask his name and Gwyn Thomas sometimes got impatient with what she called Martine's "gut" feelings. And anyway what reason would she give for her suspicions? He was a well-dressed man in a fancy car, and he hadn't done anything worse than ask who she was and remark that she didn't seem to be from around here. Martine decided to give him the benefit of the doubt. It wouldn't be the first time her instincts had been wrong.

The caracals were practically chewing the wire of their run, they were so hungry, and they crouched down, ready to pounce on their food, as Martine went into their enclosure. They had arrived at Sawubona as spitting kittens with long, fur-tipped ears, so weak and small that they'd slept on Martine's bed for the first few weeks of their existence. Now they were as muscular as young mountain lions. When she tossed their meat into the air, they leaped as if they were jet-propelled, springing eight or ten feet to claw at it and then swallowing it whole with fearsome growls.

Soon they would be ready to return to the wild. Martine knew she'd miss them terribly.

She tended to the rest of the animals with Ferris, the baby monkey, clinging to her shoulder. They all had to be fed and watered, and the dik dik, a dainty, miniature antelope with short pointy horns, needed his wound dressed. He stared up at Martine with big trusting eyes as she applied a special potion given to her by Grace, Tendai's aunt. Grace was a *sangoma,* a traditional healer of part Zulu, part Caribbean extraction. She was also the only person who knew the truth about Martine's secret gift— a gift to do with healing animals not even Martine fully understood. For that reason and many others, they had a special relationship. Now that it was school vacation, Martine was looking forward to seeing more of her.

Martine returned a protesting Ferris to his cage and headed off down the track to say good morning to Jemmy, her white giraffe. The game reserve gate was close to the house. As she let herself into the garden through a side entrance, she saw the black car still sitting in the driveway like a hearse. The chauffeur was leaning against the hood, smoking. He lifted a hand when he saw Martine crossing the yard. She waved back without enthusiasm.

Jemmy was waiting for her at the gate, just as he did every morning. He stood outlined against a kingfisher-blue sky, his white, silver, and cinnamon-etched coat shimmering in the sunshine. Martine's spirits always soared when she saw him. It was ten months since she'd tamed him and learned to ride him, but neither had lost their thrill for her. He greeted her with a low, musical fluttering sound and lowered his head. When she scratched him behind his ears and planted a kiss on his silky silver nose, his long curling eyelashes drooped in blissful contentment.

"Three more weeks of vacation, Jemmy," she said. "Can you believe that? Three brilliant weeks of no homework, no math, no history, no Mrs. Volkner ranting at me for staring out of the window, no detention; no school, period. And the best part about it is that Ben's coming to stay. It's going to be heaven on a stick. We're going to explore every inch of Sawubona in blazing sunshine and paddle in the lake and maybe even go camping."

Jemmy gave her an affectionate shove with his nose. Martine was tempted to go for a quick ride on him, but she resisted because Ben would soon be back from Cape Town and she wanted to hear about his morning. She also wanted to help him get settled into the guest room, where he'd be staying during the Christmas break while his Indian mum and African dad were away on their cruise. They'd wanted him to go with them, but Ben was studying under Tendai to be an apprentice tracker and had asked if he could stay behind to brush up on his bushcraft skills.

He and Martine were determined to have a peaceful, fun vacation at Sawubona after spending their last one trying to save a leopard from some evil hunters and a desperate gang of treasure seekers in the wilds of Zimbabwe.

Martine was locking the game park gate when the long black car suddenly *vroomed* into life. It reversed down the driveway at speed, almost knocking over a flowerpot. To Martine's surprise, her grandmother, who considered politeness to be the number one virtue and insisted in accompanying visitors out to their cars and waving until they'd gone, was nowhere to be seen. An uneasy feeling stirred in her.

She was hurrying through the mango trees toward the house when Tendai's jeep came flying into the yard. Ben was in the passenger seat. He grinned when he saw Martine, his teeth very white against the burnt-honey color of his face.

"I hitched a ride from the main road with Tendai," he explained when the jeep bounced to a halt. He hoisted his backpack over one shoulder and jumped down from the battered vehicle. He was wearing a khaki vest, baggy camouflage trousers, and hiking boots. "The people who gave me a lift seemed reluctant to come all the way to the house in case they were eaten by a lion."

Normally Martine would have cracked a joke, but she was still taking in that the house was oddly silent. At eight o'clock Gwyn Thomas was usually drinking tea and eating gooseberry jam toast at the kitchen table while listening to the news and weather on the radio. She'd also been planning to bake some scones to welcome Ben.

"Where is your grandmother, little one?" the game warden asked. "I've been calling her on both the landline and her cell phone to check with her about a delivery. There's no answer."

Martine stared at him. "Tendai, something's wrong.

This creepy man came to see her and now something's wrong, I just know it is."

"*What* creepy man?" asked Ben, dropping his backpack on the lawn.

Tendai frowned. "Are you talking of the man in the black car? He almost ran us off the road."

He started toward the house, with Martine and Ben following. Martine was kicking herself for not insisting that she go with the man to the house. If anything had happened to her grandmother . . .

Warrior, Gwyn Thomas's black and white cat, was sitting on the front step in the sunshine, his tail swishing furiously. His fur was standing on end. Tendai stepped around him and into the living room. "Mrs. Thomas?" he called. "Mrs. Thomas, are you all right?"

"Grandmother!" yelled Martine.

"No need to shout." Gwyn Thomas's subdued voice echoed faintly along the passage. "I'm in my study."

Martine flew along the corridor and knocked at the study door out of habit. Her grandmother was sitting hunched at her desk, her face the same color as the sheaf of papers she was holding. When she looked up, Martine was shocked to see that her blue eyes were rimmed with red, as if she'd been crying.

"Come in, Martine, Tendai," she said. "You too, Ben. You're part of the family."

"That weird, creepy man has done something to upset you, hasn't he? I knew he was bad news as soon as I saw him."

"Martine, how many times have I got to tell you not to judge people on the basis of your gut feelings?" Gwyn Thomas scolded. Her hands tightened on the documents. "However, in this case I fear you may be right."

She paused and gazed lingeringly out of the window, as if trying to imprint the view of springbok and zebra grazing around the water hole on her mind. "I wish I didn't have to say what I'm about to say to you all."

"Whatever it is, I'm sure it will be okay, Mrs. Thomas," Tendai reassured her.

Martine wasn't in the least bit sure things were going to be okay. "Grandmother, you're frightening us. What happened? Who *was* he?"

"His name is Reuben James," Gwyn Thomas answered at last, turning to face them. "He was a business associate of my late husband. I have a vague recollection of meeting him once and finding him a bit too flashy for my liking, although from what I remember the deal he and Henry did together went quite smoothly. Mr. James spends most of his time in Namibia and overseas and claims to have discovered only recently that Henry was killed by poachers two and a half years ago. He has just arrived with this."

She held up one of the documents. Across the middle of it was written: *Last Will and Testament of Henry Paul Thomas.* In the top right-hand corner was a wax stamp, wobbly at the corners, like a splash of blood. Peering closer, Martine made out the logo of Cutter and Bow Solicitors, Hampshire, England.

Tendai was confused. "But what is he doing with such a private document?"

"Good question. And the first one I asked him. It turns out that, three years ago, when Sawubona was in financial difficulty, Henry borrowed a large amount of money from Mr. James. He apparently agreed to change his will to say that if the money was not paid back by December twelfth of this year—today, in other words—the game reserve and everything on it would automatically belong to Reuben James."

"My God," said Tendai. He sank into the spare chair.

Martine stood frozen, the words searing a path from her brain to her heart. *The game reserve and everything on it . . . The game reserve and everything on it.*

Ben said, "Does that mean that the original will, making you the owner of Sawubona if Mr. Thomas passed away, is now worthless?"

Gwyn Thomas nodded. "Yes, because that will was written a decade or more before the one produced by Mr. James. But that's not the worst part . . ."

Martine gasped. "There's worse?"

"I'm afraid so. We've been served with an eviction order. We have thirteen days to leave Sawubona, give notice to all the staff, and say good-bye to all the animals. In thirteen days Sawubona will no longer be ours."

3

Whenever Martine thought about the fire that killed her parents—which wasn't very often because it was a no-go place in her head—one moment stood out for her. It wasn't the moment when she'd woken in a fogged-up terror on the night of her eleventh birthday to realize her home was ablaze and her mum and dad were on the other side of a burning door. It wasn't even when her room had turned into a furnace and her pajamas began melting off her back, and she'd had to improvise a rope from her bedsheets and shimmy down two stories before crashing into the snow far below.

No, it was after all of that. After she'd come rushing around the side of the house to find a crowd gathered on the front lawn. There'd been horrified gasps as people who thought she'd perished in the flames turned to see her running toward the smoldering wreckage, screaming for her parents. One of the neighbors, Mr. Morrison, had managed to catch her, and his wife had held her while she struggled and sobbed.

Martine could still remember when it hit her that her mum and dad, with whom she'd shared a laughter-filled birthday dinner of chocolate and almond pancakes just a few hours earlier, were gone forever.

That's the moment when her life had officially ended. That's when everything she'd ever loved was lost.

Now it was happening again.

The bulldozers were at Sawubona by nine a.m. the next morning. They came up the road like a line of yellow caterpillars, ready to chomp everything in their path. They parked right outside the animal sanctuary and their clunking, roaring engines terrified the sick and orphaned creatures a thousand times more than Reuben James's car had done.

Gwyn Thomas went out to stop them with an expression so ferocious that Martine was amazed their operators didn't turn tail and flee. She stood in front of the first bulldozer with her hands on her hips, like a protestor facing down an army tank.

"And what exactly do you think you're doing, coming onto my property and frightening already traumatized animals?" she demanded.

The lead operator clambered off his machine, smirking. "Just following orders, ma'am."

"You'll be following orders right into jail if you don't leave immediately. If you're not off my land in three minutes, I'm calling the police."

"Go right ahead." The man took a piece of paper from his pocket and unrolled it. "This is a court order giving us permission to start work on this site. We understand that you won't be vacating the reserve for another two weeks, but in the meantime we need to start laying the groundwork for the safari park."

"I don't care whether you're laying the groundwork for Windsor Castle," Gwyn Thomas ranted. "You're not moving one grain of sand—" She stopped. "I'm sorry. I think I misheard you. You're doing *what?*"

The man handed her the document. Gwyn Thomas put on her glasses. Martine, watching from a safe distance, saw her shoulders stiffen.

Her grandmother's voice became dangerously quiet. "The White Giraffe Safari Park? That's what you're intending to build here?"

The man's grin began to fade. "I guess so. That's what it says."

"Well," said Gwyn Thomas, "let me save you a great deal of trouble. There will be no White Giraffe Safari Park here. There will be no Pink Elephant, Black Rhino, or any other themed safari park you care to mention. Over my dead body will Mr. James inherit Sawubona."

"Now hold on a minute," objected the bulldozer operator. "There's no need for that kind of talk. I'm only doing my job."

Gwyn Thomas handed him his document with exaggerated politeness. "Of course you are. How unreasonable of me. You're only following orders. In that case you won't mind if my game warden follows orders to leave this gate open so that the lions can take their morning stroll around your bulldozers while I drive into Storm Crossing to see my lawyer? Hopefully they've already eaten their breakfast. They do love a bit of fresh meat in the morning . . ."

But Martine was no longer listening. The sick, sad feeling that had enveloped her ever since she'd learned of Sawubona's fate had been replaced by one of pure rage. The showpiece of Mr. James's grand plan to turn the game reserve into a glorified zoo was to be Jemmy. Not only was her soul mate to be taken from her, he was going to become the star of the Reuben James Show.

Trailing after Gwyn Thomas as she stalked back to the house, Martine silently echoed her grandmother's words: "Over my dead body, Mr. James."

4

Three hours later, Gwyn Thomas was back from Storm Crossing with good news and bad news.

"Tell us the nice news first," said Martine as she and Ben followed her grandmother into the study. She gestured to her friend to take the spare chair while she perched on top of a filing cabinet.

Gwyn Thomas held up a legal letter. "For what it's worth, that would be this—an injunction to prevent Mr. James and his crew of heavies from laying a single brick until the day we officially leave Sawubona: Christmas Eve. The bad news is that we can't stop them from coming to the game reserve as often as they want to in the meantime. They're entitled to bring along as many architects, designers, and wildlife experts as they feel necessary in order to plan for their takeover of the reserve."

"That's outrageous," said Martine, who didn't tend to use such dramatic words, but felt it was called for now. "We can't possibly have that hateful man planning his stupid zoo and bringing people to poke and prod our animals while we're still living here. If he lays a finger on Jemmy,

I might be tempted to do something violent. At the very least I'll have to deflate his tires."

"Martine!" Gwyn Thomas was horrified. "I will not have you talking like a young thug; I don't care how upset you are. I know you're devastated at the prospect of losing Jemmy, but really that's no excuse."

She stood up and walked over to the window. "How do you think *I* feel? Sawubona has been my home for more than half my life, and it was your mum's home before it was yours. It was your grandfather's dream before I met him and then it became our shared vision. And now I have to face the fact that the man I loved may have deceived me by signing away that dream to Mr. James."

She turned around. "But, you know, I'm not willing to believe that. Your grandfather wasn't perfect, but he was an honorable man. If he did sign away Sawubona, he'd have done it with the best of intentions—perhaps to protect me from knowing how bad our financial situation was. Either that, or he was tricked into changing his will.

"Unfortunately, none of that matters now. However noble his intentions, his actions are probably going to cost me my home and my life. And that hurts. It really hurts. Barring a miracle, Martine, in two weeks' time you and I and the cats are going to have to pack up everything we own and move into a rented apartment."

Martine tried to picture her grandmother, who loved nature more than life itself, in a poky city flat far from the wilderness of Sawubona. She was upset with herself for being so selfish. Devastated at the thought of losing her home and almost everything she loved twice in one year, she'd forgotten that it must be a thousand times harder for her grandmother.

"We can't just give up," she said. "There must be something we can do. Surely a judge would understand that a lot of the animals in the game reserve are like Jemmy. They're orphans or they've had a really horrible life and they need us to protect and love them."

Her grandmother grimaced. "Unfortunately, when it comes to property, judges tend to see things in black and white. I had hoped that the signature on the will produced by Mr. James would turn out to be a forgery, but my lawyer called in a handwriting expert and he assured us it's genuine."

Tendai knocked at the door. Gwyn Thomas ushered the game warden in with a sad smile before continuing: "No, I'm afraid there's nothing we can do."

Martine looked at Ben. He was wearing the expression he always got when the two of them were in a crisis. She could see him trying to figure out a solution.

He said, "What if there was another will—one written more recently than the one held by Mr. James—leaving Sawubona to you? Wouldn't that change everything?"

Gwyn Thomas nodded. "It would. But if there was a more recent will, Henry would have told me about it or I would have found it when I was going through his papers after . . . after he passed away."

There was an awkward silence. Nobody wanted to point out the obvious, that if Henry hadn't told her about the will held by Mr. James, he might not have told her about other things.

Martine thought about the grandfather she'd never know. He'd been killed trying to save the white giraffe's mother and father from poachers, leaving her grandmother heartbroken and without her companion of forty-two years. She said again, "We can't just give up. We have to fight."

"I agree," said her grandmother. "But I'm at a loss to think exactly how we fight."

"Would you like me to break the news about Sawubona to the game reserve staff?" offered the game warden.

"Thank you, Tendai. I couldn't face it myself, but it would be most helpful if you would."

"In the weeks before Mr. Thomas . . . passed away, did he do or say anything unusual?" asked Ben. "Did he ever seem worried or agitated?"

"Quite the reverse," Gwyn Thomas told him. "He was happier than I'd ever seen him. He was very excited about the future of the game reserve and had all sorts of projects on the go. Weeks before he died, he even made a sudden trip to England for a meeting."

She brought her hand down hard on the desk. "That's it, isn't it? Something happened on that trip. I know he was planning to see your mum and dad, Martine, but I wish I could remember what business he had there."

"When exactly did he go?" asked Martine. "Maybe you could check the date on the will produced by Mr. James and see if the two things coincided."

"I know it was during our winter," said her grandmother, "but I'd have to look in his old passport to see the exact date. I think I still have it."

She opened the bottom drawer on the right side of her desk and went through a folder. The passport was not where she'd thought it would be, so she closed the drawer again. Only it wouldn't shut properly. She wrestled with it in annoyance before wrenching it open again and feeling down the back. "Something's stuck."

She lifted out a heap of crumpled and torn bits of paper and a stiff blue envelope, a little mangled around the edges. On the front, in bold blue ink, was the word "Gwyn."

Martine was on the verge of asking if she'd like to read it in private when her grandmother seized the letter opener. She read the enclosed note and passed it to each of them in turn.

My darling,
I hope there is never any need for you to use this key. If you do it will mean I got too close to the truth. You always thought me so brave. I don't feel that way today. I hope you can find it in your heart to forgive me.
All my love always,
Henry

For several long minutes nobody said anything. Nobody knew *what* to say. It was as if Henry Thomas had spoken from the grave. At last Martine plucked up the courage to ask: "What is the key for?"

Her grandmother removed it from the envelope and examined the business card tied to it with a piece of string. "It would appear that it's for a safety-deposit box in a bank vault in England."

She slumped in her chair. "Oh, what can it all mean? What is it that I have to forgive?"

"Maybe you're right," Ben suggested. "Maybe something did happen on Mr. Thomas's trip to England."

"Perhaps. But his secret, if he had one, has gone with him to the grave."

"Not necessarily," put in Martine. "If you went to England, the answer might be in the safety-deposit box. You could do some investigating and find out what my grandfather was doing there and who he was meeting with."

Her grandmother was aghast. "I can't travel halfway across the world and leave you alone in the house, especially when Sawubona is crawling with strangers. And I'm certainly not leaving Tendai alone to face the music on the reserve. Who knows what nefarious plans Mr. James has up his sleeve."

"Martine won't be alone," Ben told her. "I'll be here to protect her."

In spite of her distress, Gwyn Thomas managed a smile. "And who's going to protect you, Ben Khumalo?"

"Why don't we call Grace and ask her if she'll come and stay for a week or two," suggested Martine. "Then Ben and I won't be alone and Tendai will have some grown-up support. One look from Grace and Reuben James will probably run for his life."

"Grace is away in Kwazulu-Natal visiting relatives," her grandmother reminded her.

"Yes, but she is back in a couple of days," Tendai pointed out. "I can have Tobias, our new guard, watch the house at night until then."

"I can't believe we're even considering this," said Gwyn Thomas. "What if it's a wild-goose chase? What if I fly thousands of miles and spend a small fortune—at a time when we can least afford it—only to discover there's nothing to discover? That the note was just something Henry wrote when he was feeling guilty about borrowing money from Mr. James."

"Then at least you'll know," Martine told her. "You'll know that there was nothing to find and you'll know that you did everything possible to save Sawubona."

But even as she spoke, a feeling of doom crept into her bones, joining the anger and dread already lurking there. "Maybe it's not such a great idea," she backtracked. "It is too far way and we'll miss you."

"No, I think you were right the first time, Martine," Gwyn Thomas said. "I should travel to England, otherwise I'll spend the rest of my life wondering if it would have made a difference if I'd only gone. I should go if it means saving Sawubona."

5

The morning after Gwyn Thomas had flown away, Sampson, an elderly game guard who patrolled the reserve on foot, radioed at six a.m. to say that he had found a buffalo needing urgent treatment for a suspected viral disease. Without that, it would die.

Martine heard the crackling of Tendai's responses and went down to the kitchen to find out what was going on. Ben had already showered and was sitting at the table drinking coffee and eating anchovy toast. In contrast to Martine, who was not a morning person and was bleary-eyed and in her pajamas, her hair sticking up on end, he looked cool, alert, and ready to face anything the day could throw at him.

"There's a sick buffalo near the northern boundary," he told Martine. "Will you come with us? We could do with your help."

Adrenaline began to course through Martine's veins. Nothing woke her up faster than an animal needing help. She took a few swallows of Ben's coffee and stole his last bit of toast, ignoring his protests. "Give me a minute," she said. She raced upstairs for her survival kit, which she never went anywhere without, threw on a pair of jeans and a blue sweatshirt, and sped outside.

As it turned out, her haste was unnecessary. Tendai and Ben were not hanging around waiting for her, they were peering under the hood of the jeep and arguing about spark plugs and fuel injectors.

"This old lady had been running since I came to work for your grandfather twenty years ago and has been patched up many times, but in between she has always been so reliable," Tendai told her. "She was working well last night. I can't think why she is refusing to cooperate this morning."

They were testing the battery when Reuben James came roaring into the yard in an open-topped Land Rover so new it sparkled.

"Perfect timing," muttered Ben.

Reuben James stepped down from his vehicle. He was crisply dressed in a white shirt and tailored khaki trousers, his bald head shining. He looked every inch the successful safari park owner. "Trouble in paradise?" he asked, strolling over to them.

He offered a hand to Tendai. "I'm Reuben James. And you must be Sawubona's famous game warden? I heard about you during my business dealings with Henry Thomas a few years ago, but I think you were away on a course at the time. You were a tracker then, if I'm not mistaken."

Without waiting for a reply, he turned very deliberately and smiled down at Martine. "We meet again."

Martine wished she had a rotten egg at hand with which to wipe the grin from his arrogant, self-satisfied face. "Unfortunately," she said.

Reuben James laughed. *"Unfortunately?* Come now, Martine, I'm sure we're going to be the best of friends."

The Zulu's jaw tightened, but he'd been taken aback by Martine's rudeness and made an extra effort to be polite. "Yes, sir, I am Sawubona's game warden. Unhappily, my jeep won't start. I will need to call the garage when they open at eight a.m. It wouldn't be a problem except that we are rushing to save a sick buffalo."

"A sick buffalo?" James waved an arm in the direction of his gold Land Rover. "Please," he said. "Take my vehicle."

They all stared at him in astonishment. Martine wondered what the catch was.

"Uh, thank you for your kind offer, Mr. James," Tendai managed, "but there is no need for that. I have friends I can telephone in an emergency."

But Reuben James wouldn't hear of it. "I insist. It would be my pleasure. My driver will be happy to escort you. Lurk, take these good people into the game reserve to find this ill creature and spend as much time there as they need. I have some paperwork to attend to that will keep me busy until you return."

He nodded toward the jeep. "In the meantime, with your permission, I'll have one of my mechanics take a look at your engine."

Before they could raise a single objection, he had ushered them into the new-leather-smelling interior of the

Land Rover, personally shutting the doors behind each of them as if he, and not the man sitting at the wheel, were the chauffeur.

As they rolled out of the yard, Martine, who was in the backseat with Ben, risked a glance behind them. Reuben James was standing in the driveway waving, just like Gwyn Thomas usually did.

It's as if he's already won, fumed Martine. It's as if he's already moved into our home. It's as if, two days after dropping this bombshell on us, he's already Sawubona's owner.

Then a little voice added: *And Jemmy's.*

The minute they were out of sight of the house, the chauffeur's ingratiating smile slipped from his face, like the moon sliding behind a cloud. He drove in sullen silence. When Tendai asked him a question about the Land Rover, he pretended he didn't understand.

They swept across Sawubona's grassy green-gold plains, and on past the lake and the high escarpment. As they drew nearer to the mountain that hid the Secret Valley, Martine felt a pang. It was months since she'd been to the white giraffe's special sanctuary. Inside the valley was a cave known only to Martine and Grace and, of course, the San Bushmen ancestors who'd recorded their lives on its walls in mystical paintings.

For reasons Martine did not even vaguely understand, they seemed to have predicted parts of her destiny there too. She could never decide whether it was a good thing or a bad thing that she had yet to figure out how to interpret the fortune-telling San paintings in the cave they called the Memory Room until it was too late. Until she'd already fallen overboard into shark-filled water, or been trapped in a cave with a wounded leopard.

"Only time and experience will give you the eyes to see them," Grace was fond of saying.

Once, when Martine had complained that it wasn't fair—that what was the point of having your destiny written on a cave wall if you couldn't use it to avoid misfortune befalling you, Grace had told her that that was precisely the point. If a person could see their future, they'd only choose the great times. "Then you would never learn and never experience the important things in this world because oftentimes they's tha hard things."

Most days Martine agreed with her. Many of her most painful experiences had led directly or indirectly to some of the most special times of her life. But even Grace would admit that losing Jemmy and every other animal Martine loved at Sawubona was not one of life's necessary experiences. Nothing good could possibly come of it.

Martine stole a glance at the twisted tree that disguised the entrance to the white giraffe's sanctuary as they went by. One night soon she planned to sneak out to the Memory Room to see if the San Bushmen had had anything to say about Reuben James stealing Sawubona. In less than a month she'd be twelve years old. Surely by now she had enough time and experience to read her own future on the cave walls?

The jeep slowed. Sampson stepped from the trees.

"Park over there, please Lurk," instructed Tendai, indicating a place on the edge of the scarred clearing. The chauffeur responded with a grunt.

"For your own safety you should remain in the vehicle," the game warden cautioned him. "We have enough problems with your boss without him suing us because some animal has given you a scratch."

Lurk gave no indication of having heard. He opened his door and jumped down. Propping himself against the side of the Land Rover, he lit a cigarette.

Tendai's eyes met Martine's. He shrugged, climbed out of the vehicle with his box of emergency veterinary supplies, and began speaking in Zulu to Sampson, a bony, wizened man who Martine was convinced was at least a hundred years old. He paused to say "Be careful" to Martine and Ben as they walked slowly into the grove of trees.

"We will," Martine assured him. Buffalo were among the most deadly of Africa's Big Five, which also included the lion, leopard, elephant, and rhino. Tourists were sometimes fooled into thinking that, because they looked like handsome dark cows with curly horns, all the fuss about how ferociously they could charge had been exaggerated. Not many of those tourists lived to tell the tale.

This buffalo, however, was no danger to anyone. He was

a young bachelor who'd probably been evicted from the main herd for fighting, but there was no fight left in him now. He was lying on his side, his streaming eyes wild and terrified, wracked with fever. As they watched he gave a great gasp, as if the life was slipping from him.

Martine's eyes filled with tears. She couldn't bear to see any animal suffer.

"Hurry, Tendai," she called, but Tendai and Sampson were involved in some sort of row with the chauffeur. He was refusing to put out his cigarette. All of a sudden he threw it in the grass. There was a shower of sparks and a dry bush on the edge of the clearing began to smolder. Sampson pulled off his shirt and thrashed at the bush. Tendai sprinted to get water out of the Land Rover, yelling at Lurk over his shoulder.

Martine eased back the buffalo's lip. The young bull's gums were almost white, a sure sign that death was approaching.

"Martine," urged Ben, "you have to do something." He, like Tendai and Gwyn Thomas, knew she had a gift with animals and wasn't really sure what that meant, but unlike them he was also aware that she had a survival kit full of special medicines and could go into a trance that would help her understand how to use them. "If it helps, I won't watch."

He was going to turn away, but Martine stopped him. "Wait," she said, "I need you to put your hands over his heart."

She took a small bottle from her pouch. When she

removed the lid, a revolting smell like frog slime, mildew, and sweaty socks tainted the air, making Ben cough.

"What *is* that stuff?" he asked, screwing up his nose. "I wanted you to help the buffalo, not gas it."

Martine paid no attention to him. She poured the green liquid into the buffalo's mouth and he revived sufficiently to sneeze, splutter, and look more dejected than ever. Laying gentle hands on the bull's head, Martine stroked his wet nose, his rough, sharp horns, and the thick, hard bone and muscle around his jaw and neck. She closed her eyes.

Time passed. Martine could not have said if it was two seconds or two hours. Her hands heated up. So fiery did they become that she almost expected them to start smoking. She heard the voices of the ancients, buzzing in her head, guiding her. The rhythm of their drums pounded in her chest. She saw great herds of giraffe and men in loincloths holding spears and . . .

"Martine, look out!"

The buffalo was surging to his feet and swinging his horns. Martine stared at him dazedly. Tendai was rushing over from the Land Rover with his rifle, and Ben was stepping in front of her protectively, at great risk to himself.

But in the end neither the rifle nor Ben's bravery were necessary. The buffalo shook his head a couple of times to clear it, snorted, and trotted away through the trees.

Tendai came running up and hugged them both in relief. "I told you to be careful. Buffalo are so unpredictable. This one even had Sampson fooled into thinking he was dying and Sampson has about a century of experience. Next time, stay with me."

"We will," said Martine, "but I don't think he had any intention of hurting us."

She avoided looking directly at Ben, but she could see out of the corner of her eye that he was very shaken. She was about to say something to take his mind off what he'd just seen when the chauffeur wandered up.

"Lurk, I told you to stay in the Land Rover for your own protection," Tendai said irritably.

The chauffeur glared at him. "I not take orders from you."

Tendai rolled his eyes. "It's not an order. It's for your own safety. Although I'm beginning to think it is the animals who need protecting from you. You almost started a bushfire."

Lurk didn't answer. He was staring over Tendai's shoulder with a peculiar, stricken expression. "Elephant!" he whispered hoarsely. "Mad elephant!"

"It's not an elephant," Tendai said irritably. "It's a buffalo. And it's not mad at all. Possibly it's a little unwell."

"Tendai," Ben said in a low voice. "He's right."

A female elephant, as vast as a baobab tree, was standing in the shadows of the forest, flapping her ears menacingly. She let out a deafening trumpet. It was clear she was about to charge.

Lurk grabbed Tendai's rifle.

"Are you insane?" shouted Tendai, trying to snatch it

back. "Do you want to get us killed? That is not a gun for elephants. The bullet will be like a bee sting for her and it will make her very, very angry."

Lurk cocked the rifle and took aim.

Tendai grabbed his wrist and crushed it so hard that Lurk winced and dropped the gun. "Don't even think about it, or I will shoot you myself. Let's all move very slowly toward the Land Rover. If she starts to charge, we must run, but be careful to run in zigzags in order to confuse her. Ready? Let's go."

They had only gone a few steps when Lurk panicked. He sprinted for the Land Rover. Martine, who'd only ever seen elephants lumbering around the water hole or trotting lazily and a little unsteadily, was stunned to see the elephant shoot from the trees like a racehorse from the stalls and gallop after the chauffeur. She gained on him rapidly. It seemed certain he would be trampled to death before he ever reached the vehicle. He'd totally forgotten about running in zigzags.

Tendai had his arms around Ben and Martine, and the three of them watched in horror. "Take off your jacket, Lurk," yelled the game warden. "Take off your jacket and throw it on the ground."

The elephant bore down on the chauffeur, her great feet tearing up the earth. In seconds, Lurk would be a bloody pulp.

"Your jacket," screamed Tendai. "Take off your jacket."

Somehow the words penetrated the chauffeur's petrified brain. He peeled off his jacket as he ran and flung it to the ground. The elephant halted in confusion. She looked from Lurk to the crumpled red pile on the ground. For an instant it seemed as if she would continue her pursuit, but then Sampson started up the engine of the Land Rover and she decided to attack the jacket instead. It was easier. Dust roiled up as she pounded it into the ground, trampling it, tossing it, crushing it.

Lurk reached the vehicle and threw himself in, sobbing. Sampson took off almost before he was seated, racing to pick up Tendai, Martine, and Ben. They scrambled in and slammed the doors. As Sampson accelerated away from the crazed elephant, swerving onto the track and gunning the engine for home, Martine heard her trumpet with rage.

6

Nobody spoke on the way back to the house. Lurk was too busy sniveling and the others were in shock. They knew they were lucky to be alive.

Martine knew that too, but it's not what she was thinking about. She was remembering the elephant's eyes. During her time at Sawubona she'd been quite close to several adult elephants and very close to a young orphan called Shaka, and the thing that had struck her was how wise and kind their brown eyes were. But the gaze of the elephant who'd attacked Lurk had been anything but. Her eyes had blazed with an unquenchable hatred. There had only been one thought in her head and that was to trample and tear to pieces the chauffeur the way she'd trampled and torn his jacket.

Lurk pulled himself together as they neared the house, and by the time Sampson drew up outside the gate and handed him the keys to the Land Rover, he was his surly self. He shot Tendai a poisonous look as he climbed into the driver's seat, but he didn't say anything. It was obvious he held the game warden responsible for his ordeal.

Tendai waited until he had driven away to collect his

employer before he said, "I think we all need a cup of tea."

Ten minutes later they were sitting around the kitchen table drinking steaming *rooibos* (red bush) tea, eating milk tart, and feeling a lot better.

"I don't understand it," Tendai said. "I've seen that elephant almost every day since she came here three years ago, and she is the shyest and most timid of all our animals. Elephants are herd animals. Their family units are very important to them, but Angel—that's what I call her because she has always been the gentlest of giants—is always alone and quick to move away. She is scared of people. But today she behaved like a bull elephant on the rampage. I'm afraid to think what would have happened if Lurk hadn't thrown his jacket on the ground."

"That was *Angel?*" said Martine, shocked. In the chaos of the moment, she hadn't paused to think which elephant was doing the charging.

There were thirteen elephants at Sawubona. Some had come in a shipment from a Zambian game reserve that had become overpopulated, several were orphans from culls, and some had been bought by her grandparents to ensure that herds were the right balances of males and females. Martine didn't know all of their histories and she couldn't really tell one elephant from another, except for two of them: Shaka, the young elephant she'd fed from a milk pail for several months, and Angel. Angel was not a regular African elephant; she was a desert elephant from Namibia, the country that bordered South Africa.

The reason she was so special to Martine was that, according to local tribesmen, Angel was the elephant who saved the white giraffe when his parents were killed hours after he was born. Somehow Angel had helped Jemmy to escape and had led him to the special sanctuary in the Secret Valley. Her own calf had been stillborn days before, so not only had she had a special affection for the grief-stricken and bewildered young giraffe, she was also able to feed him—a sight that Martine thought must have been a very extraordinary one. The two of them had been a big comfort to each other. In a way, Angel was Jemmy's adopted mother.

Riding Jemmy, Martine had been able to get within touching distance of Angel on several occasions. Like the game warden, she'd found the elephant almost painfully shy. She was always alone. She either wasn't welcome or didn't want to join the other elephants. Her only friend was Jemmy, and once he was grown she had distanced herself from even him, perhaps so that no one would guess their history. Now this seemingly angelic creature had turned on them for no reason.

"This is why I am always telling you never to take chances with wild animals," Tendai was saying. "They can change like the wind. You must never let your guard down."

"Animals are a mystery," agreed Sampson. "I would swear on the life of my nine children that that buffalo was dying of a viral disease. I was sure it was breathing its last breath when I radioed you this morning. And then it jumps up and tears away like a young calf!"

Tendai laughed. "Your eyes are not what they used to be, old man. I think you have spent so much time on your own in the bush that your imagination is playing tricks."

He pushed back his chair and put on his hat with its zebra-skin band. "I must be going. Mr. James's men might have fixed my jeep." He cast a sly look at Sampson. "Some of us have work to do."

"You call what you do work?" Sampson retorted. "You're on permanent safari." The two of them went out into the yard joshing each other and laughing.

When they'd gone, Ben regarded his friend intently and asked, "What exactly happened in the reserve with the buffalo, Martine? I mean, how did you heal it like that?"

She met his eyes with a level gaze. "It was Grace's medicine, not me. That *muti* works miracles."

And Ben accepted that because he understood that some things are better left unsaid.

"I don't know about you, but I was scared to death when the elephant charged," Martine remarked, grateful to him for not prying. "Why would Angel turn on us like that?"

"Maybe she saw or scented something that made her angry."

"You might be right. Tendai says it's true that elephants never forget. There've been studies showing that elephants can identify people from different tribes by the clothes they wear or their smell. But what could she have seen or smelled?"

"Or who?" Ben said.

Martine stared at him. "What do you mean?"

"Well, maybe she was angry at one of us."

"But why? We've only ever been loving to her." As she said it, Martine was reminded again of the hatred in Angel's eyes as she mashed Lurk's jacket into the ground.

Out in the yard, the game warden's jeep roared to life. Martine sprang up and rushed to the door. "Hey, Tendai," she called. "Where did Angel come from? I know she's a desert elephant, but how did she end up at Sawubona?"

Tendai put the jeep into gear. He seemed surprised. "I thought you knew," he said. "She was given to your grandfather by Reuben James."

7

"How 'bout offering an old woman a ride?"

Martine nearly leaped out of her skin. As anyone would if an extravagantly large medicine woman with a mixed-up Afro-Caribbean accent suddenly loomed out of the darkness at three a.m.

Martine had not intended to be in the game reserve at such an hour. Her plan had been to go to bed at nine p.m., sleep for two hours, and then go to the Secret Valley at the fairly civilized time of eleven. But she'd overslept. It had taken a considerable effort of will to haul herself out of bed when she did wake, and she'd felt a prick of conscience when she eventually let herself into the game reserve. Not about oversleeping, but about disobeying her grandmother. Under normal circumstances she was banned from riding Jemmy after nightfall. But these, Martine told herself, were not normal circumstances.

"Grace!" she cried when she'd recovered from her fright. Jemmy had bolted out of range when the *sangoma* popped up from behind a bush, but he edged closer. The Zulu woman held out her arms and Martine ran into them for a hug.

"I'm so happy to see you. How was Kwazulu-Natal? Has Tendai told you what's been going on around here? It's a total nightmare. Sawubona is going to be taken over by this businessman who claims my granddad never repaid his debt, and we all have to leave on Christmas Eve and Jemmy—"

"Relax, chile, there'll be time enough for all that later," Grace interrupted. "Right now we mus' be off to the Secret Valley."

She put a hand on one massive hip and gazed up at Jemmy's sloping white back. "Now how is old Grace supposed to get up there?"

Martine was rendered temporarily speechless. The idea of Grace, a woman who had eaten many of her own desserts, climbing aboard Jemmy, was alarming to say the least. It could do irreparable damage to the white giraffe's back. And yet she could hardly wound her friend by saying so.

Fortunately, or unfortunately, the decision was taken out of her hands. Jemmy, who was normally petrified of anyone other than Martine, made his musical fluttering sound and lay down on the ground. At which point, Grace stepped regally onto his back, settled herself as if she were relaxing into a comfortable armchair, and held a hand out to Martine. "Well, chile, are ya comin'?"

Martine couldn't refuse to join her without being rude about Grace's size, so she slipped onto the giraffe's withers, grabbed a handful of mane, and said a silent apology to Jemmy and the giraffe gods.

Jemmy staggered to his feet. Grace clutched at Martine and started gabbling fervently in Zulu. She was either swearing or praying, Martine wasn't quite sure which. At length, and going very slowly, they were on their way.

Martine's usual method of entering the Secret Valley was to grit her teeth, hold her breath, and cling as hard as she could to Jemmy's mane and back as he ran full tilt at the twisted tree and veil of thorny creepers that hid the narrow slot between the rocks. With Grace weighing him down, that was not an option, so the humans crawled through the undergrowth in an undignified fashion while the white giraffe followed more gracefully.

"The sooner ya grow up and get your driver's license, honey, the better," Grace said as she picked leaves, moss, and bits of thorn out of her headdress. "That giraffe-ridin' business is for the birds. I'll be walkin' like a rodeo cowboy for days. As for comin' into the valley through a thorn bush, it's a wonder you ain't tore all ta pieces."

"I didn't know there *was* another way." Martine switched on her flashlight and shone it around the valley, an orchid-scented space between two leaning shelves of mountain. Above them, glittering with stars, was a rectangle of blue-black sky. "How do you usually get in here?"

Grace smiled enigmatically. "I have my way, chile, and you have yours."

No matter how often she visited it, the Memory Cave

never lost its magic for Martine. Its charged air, as dense as that of a frankincense-scented cathedral, filled her lungs with history and carried her back to a time when San Bushmen painted their lives on its granite walls. Images of giraffe and men with lions' heads and great hunts and feasts chased each other in fiery shades across the cave.

She and Grace sat down on a low, flat rock that formed a natural bench. Martine was aware of Khan, the leopard she'd helped save in Zimbabwe, stealing up behind them, though she heard no sound. She could picture him stretched out on the rock behind them like a Sphinx, his golden coat with its rosettes of onyx-black shining in the torchlight. She knew he'd be watching her with an expression that was somewhere between love and confusion. Confusion—because what he felt for her went against every one of his predatory instincts.

Martine, on the hand, simply loved him.

Tears filled her eyes. Soon all of this would be taken from her. There was some satisfaction in knowing that Reuben James was unlikely ever to find this place, but that was offset by the agony of knowing she would have to say good-bye to Khan and Jemmy. Worse still, she would lose her links with the ancestors who'd written her story on the cave walls.

Grace handed her a tissue. "Tell me everythin', from the beginnin'. Leave nothin' out."

So Martine did. She told the woman she'd come to think of as a mentor, guide, friend, and earth-mother about her unsettling first encounter with Reuben James, about Henry Thomas's debt and the changed will, about Angel's attack on the chauffeur, about the discovery of her grandfather's letter with its plea for forgiveness, and about her grandmother flying away to England.

"So you see, Grace, I don't have the time to wait for experience to teach me how to read the paintings. I need an answer now. *Tonight.* We have ten days left to save Sawubona. In ten days, everything we love will be lost."

Grace took her time replying. The silence stretched out until Martine, whose nerves were at their breaking point, wanted to scream with impatience. Finally the *sangoma* heaved herself off the rock bench. She went over to what looked like a splotch on the wall and stared at it for several long minutes. Martine went to Grace's side and they studied it together.

"Surely you can't read any significance into that?" Martine said. "They probably just spilled some paint there or made a mistake."

Grace shook her head. "The forefathers did everything for a reason."

She moved off across the cave, her large palms roaming over the rock, searching for other clues. Halfway across they halted. Etched into the granite was something that looked a bit like a compass.

At once, she became agitated. "Come, chile," she said, "we mus' go."

"Go where?" Martine asked, but Grace's only answer was

to reach over and switch off Martine's flashlight. Darkness descended like a shutter.

Much as Martine adored Khan, she was wary of being in a labyrinth with the world's largest leopard when she couldn't see her hand in front of her face. But the *sangoma* had no such fears. She took Martine's hand and led her through a warren of tunnels that twisted like snakes beneath the mountain—tunnels Martine had always been much too afraid to explore on her own.

How Grace found her way in the blackness Martine had no idea, but the *sangoma* walked as if she knew these caves like she knew her own home.

The air became soupy and oppressive. Martine was beginning to feel claustrophobic and short of breath, when a sky full of stars suddenly opened up before her and sweet night air bathed her face.

They were on the mountainside above the Secret Valley. Martine was astonished to see that Khan had come with them, following at their heels like a faithful dog. His yellow gaze focused on Grace as she picked her way across the slope in the moonlight. She stopped and switched on the flashlight.

"Now do you see?" she asked.

Martine went over to her. At the foot of a large boulder, lying in a slight depression, were two great elephant's tusks. They were encrusted with dirt, as if some force had uprooted them from their usual resting place beneath the earth. Their tips were touching. They were pointing northwest.

"I see, Grace, but I don't understand. Where have they come from? How did they get here?"

The *sangoma* motioned for her to sit. Khan came and settled beside Martine, and it seemed the most natural thing in the world for her to put her arm around him. It was the first time she'd touched him since she'd saved him in Zimbabwe and it was as magical as it had been then. Warmth radiated from his golden fur. He sheathed his claws and let out a deep, contented purr.

Grace took a leather pouch from around her neck. She scattered its contents—an assortment of tiny bones, porcupine quills, a hoopoe bird feather, and fresh herbs—around the tusks, and lit a match. Her eyes closed. A spiral of incense filled the air with the scent of African violets and musk. She began to mumble loudly. Martine couldn't understand a word. It sounded as if Grace was having an argument with someone—perhaps the ancestral spirits. She was pleading with them. She crossed her arms over her chest and rocked back and forth, clearly in distress.

Martine was unnerved. She clung to Khan, unsure whether to try to wake Grace from her trance, or if that would be interfering in some sacred ritual. Khan began to growl.

Grace's eyes flicked open. She looked straight at Martine and said, "The four leaves will lead you to the circle. The circle will lead you to the elephants. The elephants will lead you to the truth."

"*What* truth?" Martine asked, and was swamped by a feeling of déjà vu. On her first morning in South Africa, she'd asked Grace that exact question. She'd been asking it ever since without ever learning the answer.

"What truth?" Martine asked again because Grace was watching her with an unreadable expression.

"*Your* truth," Grace answered. She brushed the hair from Martine's face. "When a thorn is in your heart you must pluck it out, no matter how far ya have ta go ta find the cure that will remove it."

She refused to say any more, only hugging Martine and urging her again and again to be strong. Martine rode back to the house, deep in thought. She'd offered Grace a lift on Jemmy, but the *sangoma* had turned it down, muttering something vague about having a couple of other tasks to attend to. Martine dreaded to think what tasks Grace could possibly be attending to at four in the morning in a pitch-dark game reserve, and she didn't ask any questions. Like Ben, she'd learned that some things were better left unsaid.

She was riding slowly through the game reserve, mulling over Grace's prediction, when she noticed a flare of white light on the horizon. She glanced at her watch. It was only 4:30 and still dark, but every light in the far-off house was ablaze. Either Tendai or Ben had discovered she was gone and panicked, or a drama was unfolding. Holding tight to Jemmy's mane, she urged him into a flat-out gallop.

Ben was waiting for her at the game park gate. "Go in the front door," he said quickly. "I'll keep Tendai and the guard distracted in the kitchen while you change into your pajamas. Tendai doesn't know yet that you're missing. I told him that once you're asleep it would practically take a bomb to wake you."

"Thanks," said Martine, "but if he doesn't know I'm missing, why is the house lit up like a Christmas tree?"

Ben pulled the gate shut and locked it behind her. "We've been burgled."

8

Martine stood in the middle of Gwyn Thomas's not very organized but mostly fairly tidy study and stared around in disbelief. Every drawer, box, and file was open and their contents spilled, torn, and scattered around the room. It looked as if the paper shredder had gone berserk and chewed up Gwyn Thomas's filing.

"As soon as I realized what had happened, I ran to look for Tobias," Ben was saying. "When I couldn't find him, or you, I went to Tendai's house and raised the alarm."

"This is my fault, isn't it?" said Martine. "I left the back door open when I went out riding Jemmy. It didn't enter my head that someone might break in, especially since Tobias was watching the house. I was creeping through the mango trees, thinking I'd done a really good job of evading him, when he popped up in front of me. I put my finger to my lips and he grinned."

She sank down onto the swivel chair. "Oh, Ben, what am I going to say to Tendai? I'll have to admit that I went out riding Jemmy and left the door unlocked, and he'll tell my grandmother. She's going to be livid that I've disobeyed her when she's on the other side of the world trying to save

Sawubona. She'll be so disappointed in me. She'll never trust me again."

There was a knock at the door. Tendai came in wearing a T-shirt and crumpled work trousers. He was very relieved to see Martine.

"Thank goodness you're safe, little one. When Ben told me an intruder had broken into the house, I imagined the worst—a lunatic with a machete roaming round outside your bedrooms."

"This is all my fault," Ben told him. "I heard a noise but I thought it was nothing and I rolled over and went back to sleep. It was only when I heard the gate screech that I got up and investigated. If I'd listened to my instincts sooner, none of this would have happened." He didn't add that the real reason he'd gone back to sleep was that Martine had told him she was planning to go for a late-night ride on the white giraffe and he'd assumed it was her.

"Don't take any notice of Ben," said Martine. "I'm the one to blame because I went out to see Jemmy and forgot to lock the back door."

The game warden ran a weary hand over his eyes. "It's nobody's fault and no one is to blame. If the back door hadn't been open, the burglar would have broken a window or picked the lock. He was determined to get in and nothing would have stopped him."

"But where was Tobias?" Martine wanted to know. "Did he see anyone? Did he try to stop them?"

"Tobias was knocked unconscious. He made himself a cup of tea at around three a.m., went to check on a suspicious noise near the main gate, and that's the last thing he remembers. He has a splitting headache and a lump on his head, but he should recover in a day or two. Sampson is going to take him to the hospital to be checked over by a doctor. I must stay here and wait for the police."

"Knocked unconscious? Whoever broke in must have wanted something very badly. What do you think they were after?"

"It's impossible to tell. I'm familiar with the game reserve accounts but not, of course, with your grandmother's private papers. This person left behind the petty cash, so it seems they were not after money."

"I've had a look around and nothing else seems to have been touched," said Ben. "So he or she was after something specific."

"I can't imagine who might be interested in getting his hands on my grandmother's secret papers," rtine said sarcastically.

The game warden gave her a reproving glance. "You suspect Mr. James? Please, little one, you cannot be serious. I know you are bitter about him inheriting Sawubona, as I am at the prospect of losing my job, but he is a highly respected businessman and a millionaire many times over. Respectable millionaires don't break into people's homes and ransack their studies. And why would he want to do such a thing to a house he is about to move into?"

Martine was just about to say that there was nothing respectable about millionaire businessmen who trick people into signing away their dreams, their homes, and the lives of vulnerable animals, when there was a cacophony of screaming engines and wailing sirens outside.

They all ran out into the yard. A lone police car with flashing lights was flying down the long gravel road that led from Sawubona's main entrance to the house, closely followed by an airplane that appeared to be using the road as a runway. The police car hooted at the gate just as the light aircraft shuddered to a halt in a mushroom cloud of dust. Behind the game reserve fence, a herd of springbok were springing for their lives.

Tendai shook his head. "I will admit one thing," he said. "Ever since Mr. James showed up, Sawubona has become a three-ring circus."

9

That afternoon, Martine was mopping the kitchen floor and generally trying to rid the house of the dirty bootprints, fingerprint dust, and milk tart crumbs left by the police, who'd been "worse than useless," as her grandmother would have put it, when she spotted the white giraffe at the game park gate. He seemed to be backing away. She went out onto the back *stoep* to see what was bothering him. At the far end of the garden, Reuben James was reaching up and trying to feed him through the fence.

Martine was livid. She sprinted through the mango trees and prepared to confront her nemesis.

Before she could get a word out, he said, "Ah, Martine. Nice to see you. Your giraffe—Jeremiah, is it?—and I were just getting acquainted. I hear there's a legend around here that says the child who rides a white giraffe has power over all animals. That would be you, I suppose. Lurk was telling me the other day that a buffalo that appeared to be quite dead jumped to its feet like a spring lamb when you touched it."

"I'm surprised Lurk had time to see anything," retorted

Martine. "He was too busy trying to start a wildfire with his cigarette, being rude to Tendai, and frightening our elephants."

Reuben James chuckled. "I rather think that it was the elephant who frightened him. In my experience, elephants are much hardier than people would like to believe. Look at the one I gave to your grandfather. She was skin and bone and could hardly put one foot in front of the other when she arrived here, and now I'm told she's as right as rain. Nothing wrong with her at all."

Martine wondered if he had made the connection that the elephant he'd given Sawubona was the same one who'd charged his chauffeur. She decided not to say anything in case he hadn't. He might decide to punish Angel when he took over the reserve.

Realizing he could do the same to Jemmy if she upset him, she said more politely, "Would you mind leaving my giraffe alone and not feeding him? He's nervous of strangers and he only eats acacia leaves."

Reuben James craned his neck to squint at Jemmy, who was hovering near the fence to be close to Martine. "Oh, I'm sure he could be tempted with a treat or two." He held up a sprig of honeysuckle flowers.

The white giraffe leaned toward him, his mouth watering at the sight of such a delectable dish, but his terror of the man was too strong and he pulled back without taking any.

Martine wanted to scratch Reuben James's eyes out. Controlling herself with difficulty, she let herself into the game reserve, shutting and locking the gate behind her just to prove that she still had rights at Sawubona and he didn't. Jemmy put his head down and nuzzled her.

From the other side of the fence, Reuben James said smoothly, "I hear you had a break-in last night."

"And I suppose you had nothing to do with it?" snapped Martine, forgetting her resolution to be polite.

He smiled. "Come now, Martine, you and I seem to have got off on the wrong foot. It's hardly surprising that you've taken against me, given how much you love Sawubona, but breaking and entering is really not my style."

"Oh, and taking away people's dreams and wildlife sanctuaries is?"

Reuben James tossed the honeysuckle on the ground and wiped his hands on a monogrammed handkerchief. "Martine, you're too young to understand about business, but ask yourself this. If your grandfather had cared, *really* cared about Sawubona, would he have overstretched himself financially and put his family's future in jeopardy? I think not. I'm not the bad guy here."

She had to hand it to him—he was good. For a moment, he almost had *her* questioning what Henry Thomas had done. But then he went too far.

He leaned against the fence and said, "I tell you what, Martine, I'm prepared to make a deal with you. Choose an animal, any animal, on the reserve, and it's yours. You can visit it for free whenever you want to. Any animal, that is, except the white giraffe. Did I tell you we're planning to change Sawubona's name to the White Giraffe Safari Park in his honor?"

At the mention of the safari park, a cold calm came over Martine. She saw that she and Reuben James were like chess players. He had made his move and now she had to make hers. An image of Grace navigating her way bravely through the catacombs of the Secret Valley entered her mind. She said, "You know, you really shouldn't underestimate us. There are people at Sawubona who have powers you couldn't possibly understand."

Her green eyes met his blue ones in challenge. "Somehow we're going to find a way to stop you."

Something dark and almost savage flitted across Reuben James's face, but it was gone before Martine could take it in. His customary polished smile replaced it.

"Is that a fact?" he said. "Well, let me give you a word of advice, young lady. I'm a patient man and a generous one, but I'm only patient and generous to a point. Don't make the mistake of crossing me."

The phone was ringing when Martine walked back into the house. She picked up the receiver in the kitchen. Outside, the wind was heavy with the iron scent of rain, and the back door creaked on its hinges. Battleship-gray clouds scudded over the game reserve.

"Martine, thank goodness I've reached you," cried Gwyn Thomas. "I've been calling and calling but there's been no reply. I've been worried sick. What's going on there? Is everything all right?"

"Everything's fine," lied Martine. There was no point telling her grandmother about Lurk being charged by the elephant or the burglary or anything else. She'd only freak out and do something drastic like get on the next plane home without having discovered anything at all in England. Sawubona would be more in jeopardy than ever. "Sorry you've had trouble getting hold of us. Grace doesn't like to answer the phone and Ben and I have been out on the reserve a lot, helping Tendai."

"Well, thank goodness for that. I was imagining the worst. Has Mr. James been back?"

"Back and forth, but we can handle him," Martine replied, and changed the subject. "How's England? Is it freezing?"

"And gray," confirmed her grandmother. "And very wet. I'm staying at a country inn straight out of a werewolf movie, with low beams and hostile locals and its very own Hound of the Baskervilles. The room is so small I have to climb into bed as I come through the door. But that's not what I called to talk to you about."

"The key!" Martine said, remembering. "What was in the safety-deposit box? Did you find a different will?"

"Not exactly. To be honest, it's all a bit mysterious and it's left me questioning my sanity. I'm wracked with guilt about abandoning you, Ben, and Tendai to the mercy of that awful man in order to fly thousands of miles on what appears to be a wild-goose chase. The safety-deposit box contained nothing much of anything, really. Certainly nothing that's going to help us save Sawubona. Just an envelope."

"An envelope? Is there a letter in it?"

"No, that's the peculiar part. There were only two items in it: a map of Damaraland in Namibia, and another key. The type that might fit a suitcase lock."

"What suitcase?"

"Your guess is as good as mine. The other thing that's strange is that the envelope is one that belonged to Veronica."

"My mum?"

"I was surprised too," said Gwyn Thomas. "It has your old Hampshire address on the back in her handwriting. I can't think what it's doing in Henry's safety-deposit box."

"Maybe she had something she needed to keep safe?" Into Martine's mind, unbidden, came the thought: *Or maybe she had something to hide.*

"An African tourist map and a key with no address label on it? No, I think it's more likely that whatever she or Henry put in the box has long since been removed and that the map is just a stray memento from some trip or other. The key might be worth looking into, but without an address, I don't really know where to start."

They talked about things closer to home after that. Gwyn Thomas missed Sawubona and everyone on it and wanted an update on almost every animal on the reserve. That roused Martine's suspicions immediately. If there was one thing her grandmother couldn't abide it was wasted money, especially when it came to the telephone, and she was sure the call from England was costing a fortune. And yet every time she tried to say good-bye, her grandmother would find a new way to keep her on the line.

After five or six minutes of this, Martine said, "Is there something on your mind, Grandmother?"

"No, of course not. Well, naturally I'm very concerned about the future, but apart from that I'm fine. I should go. I'm sure my phone card is about to run out. They're a con these cards, an absolute con."

Martine carried the phone over to the kitchen window. Through it she could see the length of the garden and all the way down to the water hole on the other side of the game fence, over which a black sky hung low. Six pot-bellied zebras were trotting for cover. Martine said, "Are you afraid of what you might find if you start investigating?"

The voice on the other end of the line was indignant. "Afraid? Don't be ridiculous." There was a pause and then Gwyn Thomas said, "Oh, who am I kidding? Yes, Martine, to be honest, I am scared. I'm scared that the man I loved, the man whose life I shared for forty-two years, might not have been the man I thought he was."

There was a rush of wind through the mango trees. Fat drops began to fall, drumming the thatch. The roses bowed their heads as the rain fell faster and faster.

"My heart tells me that he was a good, kind man who would never have done anything to hurt me, but at the back of my mind is the nagging doubt that you can never truly know another person . . ." The rest of the sentence was drowned out by the rain, which was now coming down in sheets.

Martine cupped her hand over one ear, straining to hear. The line crackled and hissed. She hit the button that switched it to speakerphone.

Her grandmother's disembodied voice burst into the kitchen, echoing around the appliances. "Secrets destroy, Martine. Never keep one. Henry's secret mission, however noble, might mean the end of Sawubona and everything I've ever worked for and love. I have no wish to depress you, but you're going to have to face the fact that it could also mean the end of the white giraffe."

10

Dinner that night was a subdued affair. Grace cooked and the food was as delicious as ever, but nobody had any appetite. Ben sat racking his brains for a solution to the situation at Sawubona. For years he'd been an outcast, shunned and bullied at school, but Martine, her grandmother, Tendai, and Grace had changed his life. They'd not only welcomed him into their world and accepted him for who he was, with no reservations, they'd helped him to follow his dream of working in nature and with wildlife. Now they needed *his* help and he was frustrated that he'd so far been unable to think of any way he might provide it.

Martine pushed her food around her plate, feeling blue. It was difficult to enjoy even a meal such as this—fresh bream caught by Sampson in the game reserve lake, accompanied by roasted cherry tomatoes, sweet potato mash, and African spinach, with a lemon meringue pie to follow. Every meal at Sawubona now had a "Last Supper" tone to it.

The phone call had left her deeply concerned about her grandmother. She was accustomed to Gwyn Thomas's feisty confidence, the kind that had allowed her to face down the bulldozer operator without blinking. It distressed her to hear her grandmother sounding so vulnerable and afraid.

Grace watched her without saying anything, but after the meal she took Martine aside and presented her with a small parcel wrapped in brown paper.

"What's this for?" Martine asked in surprise.

Grace smiled. "I been thinkin' that ya mus' be runnin' low on Grace's special *muti*. Last night, after ya went away on your giraffe, I went to find some special herbs and some plants for you."

Martine hardly knew how to respond. The thoughtfulness of the *sangoma* touched her to the core.

Added to which, Grace was right. The traditional remedies Martine kept in her survival kit were almost finished. She'd used the last drop of the medicine Grace laughingly called "Love Potion No. 9," after a song she'd heard, on the buffalo. Martine wasn't sure (and didn't care to know) what the tiny brown bottles of *muti* contained, but Grace always wrote a detailed list of symptoms they were meant to treat on their labels. And, boy, were they effective.

She went to open the brown paper parcel, but Grace stopped her. "Not now," she said. "There'll be time enough for that tomorra. Put it away in your survival kit."

After the events of the day, sleep was not an option for Martine, particularly since the caracals were sleeping on her bed. Tendai had decided they'd be more effective than any human at guarding the house, and Martine and Ben agreed.

Unfortunately, it was a sweltering night and the caracals made Martine even hotter. She tossed and turned, her heart aching at the thought of life without Jemmy, who, she was sure, would not understand that she'd been forced to leave him to the mercy of Reuben James and the tourist hordes who would descend on the new White Giraffe Safari Park. He'd feel abandoned and betrayed.

At 2:30 a.m. she could stand it no longer. She got up, took a quiet shower so as not to wake Ben and Grace, dressed, and went down to her grandmother's study, followed by the caracals. Tendai had tried to tidy up some of the papers, but the room still looked like a tornado had blown through it. Martine picked through the mess until she found what she was looking for: the logbook for Sawubona's wildlife. Her grandmother and grandfather had always kept meticulous records of the history of each animal.

She found Angel easily enough, though the elephant hadn't had a name back then. Her grandfather had written her entry in bold blue handwriting.

Female desert elephant, approx 10 yrs old, 22 months pregnant, donated by Reuben James, who rescued her from a zoo in Namibia, extreme case of neglect, v. thin, covered in rope burns and untreated sores, grave concerns for health of her unborn calf.

It was a tragic story, and one that brought tears to Martine's eyes. She wondered if she'd misjudged Reuben James. Perhaps his takeover of Sawubona was just that—business. Fair compensation for the non-payment of a debt. Perhaps he genuinely did care for animals and would continue to rescue them when he was running his own safari park. Then she remembered that he was planning to exploit the white giraffe and was angry at him all over again. She was glad he'd saved Angel from the cruel zoo in Namibia, but nothing would make her like him.

She glanced again at her grandfather's notes on Angel and a line naming the elephant's place of birth caught her eye: Damaraland, Namibia.

For a moment Martine couldn't think where she'd heard the name before, but then she remembered her grandmother's call. There'd been nothing in the safety-deposit box, Gwyn Thomas had told her, except a map of Damaraland. It was an odd coincidence. And Grace always said that there was no such thing as a coincidence.

Martine went over to the bookcase and took down a guidebook on travel in Africa. She flicked through it to the Namibia section. Damaraland was in the north of the country. It was, the book explained, the home of Namibia's highest mountain, the oldest San etchings in Africa, and the rare and elusive desert-adapted elephant. These were taller than regular African elephants, with long legs capable of carrying them forty-five miles a day. Ordinary elephants drink twenty-five to fifty gallons of water a day, but desert elephants could survive even if they only consumed this amount every three or four days.

Martine returned the book to the shelf and switched off the lamp. Restless, she went out into the garden to see if she could see Jemmy, taking the caracals with her for protection. She didn't fancy being hit over the head by any burglars. The white giraffe was not at the water hole. Martine was debating whether to return to the house for the silent whistle she used to call him, when a different glimmer of white caught her eye: Reuben James's plane.

At dinner, Ben had mentioned that he'd overheard the pilot saying he had orders to have the aircraft ready at five a.m. He and Reuben James were returning to Namibia, James's home. They had no plans to return until Christmas Eve, when they officially took over Sawubona. It was the first good news Martine had heard in a week.

Switching on her flashlight, she went over to the plane. It was a Beechcraft B58. There were six seats and a section for cargo at the back. She walked around to the aircraft's nose. Its name was on its side in bold red letters: *Firebird*. Beneath it, so small that you'd only notice it if you were standing right beside it was . . .

Martine got such a surprise that she dropped the flashlight. It rolled under the wheels and it took a minute for her to find it again. She shined it at the nose of the plane. Beneath the Firebird banner was a four-leaf clover.

"The four leaves will lead you to the circle," Grace had told her.

Martine sat down on the rock near the gate. The caracals milled around her, wanting attention. Reuben James was flying to Namibia, a country that just happened to be northwest of Sawubona, the direction the elephant tusks had been pointing. The map in the safety-deposit box had been of Damaraland, and Damaraland just happened to be the birthplace of Angel.

A plan started to take shape in Martine's head. What if she were to hitch a ride with Mr. James and take a look at whatever it was he was up to on his travels? Maybe she could find a bit of dirt on him—some proof that he was a corrupt businessman who'd tricked her grandfather into giving away the game reserve? At the same time, she could try to follow the clues in Grace's prophecy.

Other, more sensible thoughts crowded into her mind. Thoughts such as: Are you *nuts?* You could be killed. You could be sent to jail or a youth offenders' institute or wherever it is they send eleven-year-olds who stow away on planes to foreign countries. Oh, and if Reuben James doesn't shoot you, your grandmother will when she discovers what you've done.

But it was no use. If Martine listened to the rational part of her brain, it would mean sitting idly by while James turned Sawubona into a petting zoo for tourists who fancied a ride on a white giraffe. It would mean allowing her grandmother's home to be snatched away; Ben's dream of being a tracker to go up in smoke; and Tendai, Sampson, and all the other Sawubona staff to be out on the street with no jobs.

Worse still, it would mean finding a sign that Grace

had told her would lead her to the "truth," whatever that meant, and ignoring it. For all of those reasons, the brave and crazy part of her was willing to throw caution to the wind.

Martine decided to submit herself to one final test. Realistically, the only way she'd be able to stow away on the plane would be to do it tonight, under cover of darkness. And she could only do that if the door had been left unlocked. She tried the door.

It was unlocked.

Martine exhaled in a rush of breath. So that was decided. She had to do this thing now, whether she wanted to or not. She checked the time again. It was two fifty. She needed to be on board by four a.m. at the latest.

Ignoring the objections that piled into her mind, she returned to the house. After packing her survival kit, Windbreaker, a spare T-shirt, extra socks and underwear, and her toothbrush into a small backpack, she went down to the kitchen and filled a lunchbox with two cheese and apricot chutney sandwiches and a bottle of water. She left a note on the kitchen table.

Dear Grace

I've gone to pluck out the thorn. Please take care of Jemmy and the sanctuary animals and do what you can so that my grandmother doesn't worry.

I love you all.

Martine xxx

66

As she left the house, shutting the caracals in behind her, she cast a wistful glance at Ben's bedroom window. She didn't know how she'd manage without her best friend, but it wasn't fair to involve him in such an irresponsible scheme.

Clicking the door shut behind her, she sprinted for the gate. There she paused and listened. Apart from the night creatures, there wasn't a sound. Heart pounding, she climbed into the plane and lay down behind the boxes in the hold, a tarpaulin covering her. She couldn't believe how easy it had been.

She was settling down for a nap, using her backpack for a pillow, when she heard a noise. She tensed. It was highly unlikely that Reuben James was making preparations to leave at three forty-five a.m., which meant that someone— with her luck it would be Lurk—had spotted her getting onto the plane. And that was a disaster.

The door hissed open. Martine shrank into her dark corner, trying not to breathe. Terror paralyzed her. The seconds ticked by. Her chest began to burn with lack of oxygen.

Just when she thought she'd either have to breathe or explode, the tarpaulin lifted. Ben grinned down at her. He was dressed and carrying the small khaki pack he took with him when he was tracking. Martine was still spluttering for words when he crawled in beside her.

"You didn't think I was going to let you go on your own, did you?" he said.

11

Martine had a cramp. It had started in her foot and spread up her calf and now she had to bite down on her sweatshirt to stop from crying out. She was also freezing, starving, and thirsty, and somehow her cold, hunger, and dry mouth were made that much worse by the knowledge that her Windbreaker, sandwiches, and the bottle of water were within touching distance, only she couldn't get to them. Not without attracting the attention of the pilot or Reuben James. Not without risking discovery.

She huddled closer to Ben and managed to straighten her leg enough to ease the pain. They'd been flying for close to three hours. At 4:30 a gust of cold air had alerted them to the opening of the plane door and the lights had flicked on. It had seemed impossible she and Ben wouldn't be caught, but the pilot merely slung a couple of suitcases on top of them and started up the engines. Minutes later, they heard Reuben James's shouted greeting. Another box was piled into the cargo area and then they were bumping down the makeshift runway and taking off into the unknown.

And now what?

That was the question that had occupied Martine's mind for the best part of the journey. As usual, she hadn't thought that far ahead. Now that she'd had time to reflect on her actions, regret had been added to the list of emotions she'd experienced over the past few days. She and Ben were about to enter a foreign country without passports. Without anyone knowing where they were. Without a plan. And without money. She had a handful of loose change with her, but it was hardly enough for a hamburger. How on earth would they ever get back to Sawubona?

All she knew about Namibia were the facts she'd gleaned from the guidebook. That it was one of the most sparsely populated countries on earth, with only 1.8 million people occupying 309,000 square yards. That it was home to some of the last nomadic, herding tribes in Africa, the most ancient of which were the San Bushmen. That 60 percent of Namibia was made up of the deserts of the Kalahari and the eighty-million-year-old Namib, and that December was one of the hottest months of the year there, with temperatures climbing into the 100s.

Martine began to feel more panicky by the minute. She'd dragged her best friend into this. She'd left Grace to deal with Gwyn Thomas, although, since Grace had all but given her permission to travel as far as she needed to, Martine didn't feel quite so bad about that. Her main concern was her grandmother. With any luck Gwyn Thomas wouldn't phone for a few days, by which time Martine and Ben would be safely back at Sawubona.

She hoped.

Martine became aware that the aircraft was descending. Her ears popped. She nudged Ben awake, marveling that he was able to sleep at such a time. His eyes opened and he stared around in confusion before recalling where he was. He smiled at Martine and, as always, that made her feel better. At least she wasn't alone. At least she and Ben were together.

The ground rose unexpectedly to meet them, slamming into the plane's underbelly. They bounced and shuddered to a halt. The engines shut down and all was quiet.

"A textbook landing, even if I say so myself," remarked the pilot. "Not far to go now. We'll refuel and clear customs and be on our way. Bet you'll be relieved when this is all over."

"Right now, I'm most relieved about being away from Sawubona," responded Reuben James. "It was bad enough when that old battle-axe Gwyn Thomas was around, but her granddaughter is much more disconcerting. She has these green eyes that look right into your soul, like X-rays. She threatened me yesterday, basically said that there were people on the game reserve who had powers I couldn't possibly understand, and that they'd stop me."

He chuckled. "The idea that this skinny little kid or one of the game reserve staff could stick pins in a voodoo doll or stir up a magic potion to prevent me from fulfilling a plan that's been years in the making is a joke, but she said it in a way that almost had me believing it."

"What are you going to do about her?" asked the pilot, but before the other man could answer, a customs official was at the window. The next few minutes were taken up with administration and refueling.

After that the plane took off again and flew for another forty-five minutes. By then, Martine was so desperate for the bathroom she was prepared to give herself up in order to go. Fortunately the plane began its descent as she was trying to communicate this to Ben. They touched down shortly afterward.

"I'm glad this is our last journey with this type of cargo," said the pilot when the engines had shut down. "I don't think my nerves could stand another one. If that customs official had searched the plane, my life would not have been worth living."

"Think of your Swiss bank account," Reuben James reminded him.

"It's not going to be much use to me if I'm behind bars."

"You should have thought about that sooner. In any case, we're not breaking the law, merely bending it. As Callum always says, we're performing a national service."

"Do you think the . . . will see it that way?" Martine missed the word or name because a vehicle drove up outside.

"Sure they will," said Reuben James. "Where else are they going to get access to three square meals and fresh water every day?"

He and the pilot greeted the driver of the vehicle and

the pair of them clambered out of the plane. An engine revved and faded into the distance.

Martine and Ben climbed stiffly to their feet. They opened the door cautiously and stepped out into a wall of heat.

As far as they could see there was nothing but desert. Not a desert with rippled gold sand, but one with sky-scraping red dunes. It rose around them in mountain-ous peaks of burnished umber, sculpted by the wind into knife-edged cliffs, ravines, and valleys, and thrown into sharp relief by the morning sun. It was a scene of immense beauty, but it was a desolate one.

Martine felt faint. She put a hand on the wing of the plane. Ben met her gaze and she could tell he was thinking the same thing. They were alone in the desert, thousands of miles from home, with two cheese sandwiches and a bottle of water.

12

"Now what?" said Martine. It was a relief to say the words out loud after lying on the shuddering floor of the plane for several hours thinking them.

Ben ran his fingers through his black hair. "Good question. What's the first rule of survival in any situation?"

"Don't panic."

"So let's not panic. Before we move, let's go over the plane inch by inch and see if there is anything on it that might be of use to us. First, though, we should eat something."

They shared the sandwiches and half the bottle of water, reasoning that the cheese would melt and go moldy in the heat and then it would be no use to anyone. After that, they returned to the plane and examined its contents meticulously.

There wasn't much *to* find, particularly since they couldn't remove anything that would be missed. They did take two small cartons of juice from a cool box, and some glucose and water-purification tablets and a blanket from the first aid box, but they drew the line at going through the suitcases.

"Innocent until proven guilty," Ben said. Martine was of the opinion that Reuben James was guilty until proven innocent, but she agreed that going through his belongings should be a last resort.

They did investigate the cargo in the hold. Most were boxes, tightly sealed, but the name of the manufacturer on the exterior and the smell coming from one with a missing corner made Ben fairly certain they were mining supplies.

"Mining supplies?" said Martine. "Is that how Reuben James is making his millions then? From diamonds or platinum?"

"I'm not sure. I asked Tendai about it and he thought James was in the business of developing luxury tourist lodges. But he didn't really know."

He shoved the boxes back into position and the two of them hopped out of the plane and closed the door. Martine caught sight of the four-leaf clover on the belly of the aircraft again and remembered Grace's prophesy.

The four leaves will lead you to the circle. What circle?

"Could you make any sense of the conversation on the plane?" she asked Ben. "What do you think Reuben James meant when he said that they were not breaking the law, just bending it? Who's Callum? And what was all that talk about Swiss bank accounts and jail? The pilot said that if the customs officer had searched the plane his life would not have been worth living. So they must be doing something at least a bit illegal."

"It was when Mr. James made out that someone, somewhere, should be grateful that they were getting three square meals and water every day that I really started worrying. It almost sounded as if he was referring to slave labor. It's all very mysterious, but I think we can be certain of one thing."

"What's that?"

"This is about something much bigger than Sawubona."

They had no way of knowing when the pilot and/or Reuben James would return to collect the cargo, but they guessed that at the very least the men would be off eating breakfast somewhere. And it was vital that they try to get their bearings before it got any hotter. They were uncomfortably conscious of how little liquid they had.

Within minutes of starting to climb the dunes, Martine would have killed for something sweet, fizzy, and ice-cold. She and Ben were barefoot, having taken off their boots and slung them around their necks, and their toes sank deep into the red sand. On and on they slogged, muscles burning. Halfway up, they shared the remainder of the water. Neither of them said anything, but both of them knew that once the apple juice was gone they'd be in trouble.

"I bet you we get to the top and find there's a lovely hotel with shady palms and a sparkling blue swimming pool on the other side," Ben said hopefully.

"I bet you we get to the top and there's an air-conditioned

shopping center offering free chocolate chip ice cream and all the lemonade we can drink!" said Martine.

That cheered them up and they resumed their struggle to the top of the dune. Ben, who was a lot fitter than Martine, made it there first, with a lot less panting. She joined him a minute later, but took her time getting her breath back before looking around. Ben's expression had already told her what she was likely to see, and she was in no hurry to have it confirmed.

From horizon to blue horizon stretched layer upon layer of red dunes, tossed and scooped like some gigantic desert dessert. There was no sign of life. Had it not been for a tar road that tapered away in the haze, and the plane, toy-sized on the distant runway, they could have been on Mars.

"If it helps, we're in Sossusvlei," said Ben. "I recognize these red dunes from photographs. We're at least six hours by car from the nearest big town."

"Great," said Martine, shielding her eyes from the glaring sun. "Let's hope we don't have to do it on foot."

She sat down on the dune. "Ben, I'm so sorry. As usual, this is my fault. I was in such a state at the possibility of losing Jemmy and Khan and Sawubona, I wasn't thinking clearly. I was sick of feeling helpless. I wanted to do something. It didn't occur to me that Reuben James would be doing business in the middle of the Namib desert. I thought we'd be in a proper place with cars and roads and houses, where I could do some investigating. But this is a disaster. And the worst part is, I've dragged you into it."

Ben flopped down beside her and opened one of the little cartons of apple juice. He offered it to her before taking a sip himself. "You didn't drag me into it. I came because I wanted to, remember? Anyway, you need to take your own advice."

"What advice is that?"

"What you said to your grandmother. We can't give up. Let's do what we came here to do. Let's get to the bottom of what Reuben James is up to and find enough evidence to prevent him from taking over Sawubona."

Martine looked at him. "There's something else."

Briefly, she told him about Grace's prophesy, about the northwest-facing tusks and finding the four-leaf clover on the belly of the plane. She also relayed her grandmother's conversation about the Damaraland map in the safety-deposit box, and told him of the strange coincidence of Angel being from that exact place. "Grace always says that there's no such thing as a coincidence. So it's a bit odd to find two sets of coincidences in less than twenty-four hours."

"Mmm," murmured Ben. "And there might be a third. What if the reason Angel attacked Lurk was that she knew him from Damaraland and that he did something to anger her back then? I think we owe it to Angel, your grandmother, and everyone else at Sawubona to investigate this a bit further. We need to find a way to Damaraland."

For the first time in days Martine felt hope stir in her veins. "Okay," she said. "Let's do what we've come here to do. We've been in worse situations than this. Let's hide near the plane until they return for the cargo and then see if we can sneak into their vehicle."

They soon found that the easiest way down the steep dunes was to slip-slide on their behinds as if they were tobogganing. Descending was a whole lot more fun than going up. They were almost at the bottom when they spotted a swirl of dust on the road. The safari vehicle was returning.

They were completely exposed on the slope and hundreds of yards from the nearest cover, so they skidded to a halt where they were and buried themselves in the powdery red earth until only their heads were showing. Below them, the safari vehicle halted beside the aircraft. The pilot and Reuben James unloaded several long wooden crates, hoisted them onto the plane, and climbed in after the cargo. Five minutes later, they still hadn't emerged. The propellers on the plane started whirring.

"They're leaving!" cried Martine, half sitting up. "Ben, they're leaving us! I assumed that this was their final destination and we'd have ages to return to the plane. I thought Reuben James either lived near here or had business around here, and that the plane wouldn't be going anywhere for days."

"So did I," said Ben grimly. "I guess we assumed wrong."

The drone of the engine grew louder as the pilot prepared for takeoff. The driver of the safari vehicle waved and sped away.

Martine and Ben watched as the white aircraft taxied

down the runway and shot into the blue. Moments later, the sky was empty. It was as if the plane and the men on it had been a figment of their imagination.

A silence in which the only sounds were the whisper of sand and their own short, frightened breathing seemed to swoop down and chill them, in spite of the heat of the day.

"Now what?" said Ben.

13

"STOP," said Martine.

In everyday life she was quick to anger and quick to cry and she definitely felt like doing both now, but when faced with a survival crisis she'd learned the importance of listening to her head and not her heart.

Ben stared at her in surprise. "Stop what?"

"STOP. It's an anagram for Stop, Think, Observe, Plan. I read about it somewhere. It's a way of staying focused and not having a meltdown when you're in a really desperate situation."

"Which we are," Ben said with feeling. "A *really* desperate situation."

Martine stood up and shook red sand from her clothes and cropped brown hair. "In a way, this might be a blessing."

"How's that?"

"Well, supposing we had been on board that plane. Odds are, the longer we were around Reuben James, the more chance there was of us getting caught. All it would have taken is for one of us to sneeze. But now we're free agents. We're in Namibia and on his trail, but we get to say how and when we do things."

Ben burst out laughing. "Boy, have you changed over the past year. But you're totally right. We're a zillion miles from anywhere and boiling alive in the desert sun with one tiny carton of apple juice and no transport. We have to think positively if we're going to get out alive. Okay, let's get on Mr. James's trail. But first we need shelter, water, and food—in that order."

"I agree. Ben?"

"Yeah."

"Deep down, I'm terrified, you know. I don't think I've ever been so scared in my life. But I'm also very determined. I'm going to save Sawubona and all our precious animals if it's the last thing I ever do."

Ben looked from her to the endless cliffs of burning red sand and back again, his dark eyes serious. "Let's hope it's not," he said.

The most critical course of action was for them to escape from the sun. Since there was no shelter of any kind for miles and they could not risk getting dehydrated searching for one in the fierce heat, they returned to the airstrip and rigged up a canopy using the blanket. They stayed there until mid-afternoon, dozing and daydreaming about food and icy drinks. The apple juice had been finished by lunchtime. With the last of it, they used a survival trick, keeping it in their mouths for as long as they could so that their tongues and lips didn't dry out.

Late afternoon, they ate a glucose tablet each and set off

into the energy-sapping heat. They had hoped the airstrip might be in regular use and they'd soon be rescued, but they never saw a soul. Both of them knew that in a lot of survival situations it was best to stay where you were until you were rescued rather than move and make your situation worse, but, since nobody was aware they were in need of rescuing, it was up to them to seek help.

They followed the road in the direction the safari vehicle had taken earlier that morning. It was a lot less strenuous than climbing the dunes, and there was always the chance that a busload of tourists or a park warden with a vat of water on board would drive by. That was their hope, at any rate.

It didn't happen.

As the hours ticked past and the sun slipped lower in the sky, Martine's mouth became so dry that her tongue kept sticking to the roof of it, and her lips cracked and bled a little. She'd put on her Windbreaker and pulled up the hood to protect her from sunburn, but all it did was make her hotter. Her limbs weakened. She put one foot in front of the other and tried not to think of the stories she'd read about people dying in the desert. The longest the body could go without water was three days. In this heat, a person could be dead in twenty-four hours.

Her biggest concern was that they might be walking in the wrong direction. The safari vehicle might not have been heading for a tourist lodge at all. If Ben was right about the contents of the boxes, it could have been taking Reuben James to a mine or perhaps a secret storage unit.

There might be armed guards there. She and Ben might be walking into a trap.

A lizard with a snout like a shovel shot streaked across a nearby dune with a swimming motion. Apart from beetles and a distant eagle, it was the only sign of life they'd seen all day.

"We're not going to die," Martine said out loud with a lot more confidence than she felt. "Grace would have mentioned it if we were."

"She might have left that part out, so as not to alarm you," Ben teased. "Don't fortune-tellers abide by some sort of code where they don't tell people if they see something ghastly?"

Martine suddenly felt exceedingly hot and irritable. "That's really not helpful, Ben," she said crossly. "Anyway, Grace is not a fortune-teller. She's a *sangoma* who can commune with the spirits and read the bones. It's not like she's some charlatan with a sequined vest and a crystal ball."

Ben stopped. "Hey, I know that. Grace is completely amazing. I'm sorry, it was a stupid thing to say. I was trying to keep things light, that's all."

Martine squeezed his hand. "Sorry I snapped at you. I'm just hungry and tired and I keep blaming myself for the mess we're in."

Ben grinned. "That doesn't sound like positive thinking to me. Come on, we can do it. Quick march, quick march, quick march . . ."

Sunset brought a breeze so cool and soothing it was like

being wrapped in silk. Martine and Ben used the last of their strength to climb the highest dune in the area, where they hoped they'd be out of reach of predators, snakes, and scorpions during the long night ahead. They were also hoping to catch a glimpse of a tourist lodge or some indication of water.

Before they climbed, they removed their shoes again. The warm red sand slipped through Martine's toes. Close to the top, they paused for breath. The sunset did not have the exotic hues of those Martine saw regularly at Sawubona, but the colors of the desert made up for it. Bathed in the pure light of evening, the great rippled dunes turned every shade of brick red, burnt orange, and chestnut brown.

It was a sight so lovely, so lonely, and so ancient that Martine momentarily forgot their plight and felt lucky to be witnessing it. According to the guidebook, the Namib Desert was an estimated eight hundred million years old. In terms of evolution, she was about as insignificant as an amoeba. She lingered on the slope even after Ben began to climb again, only emerging from her reverie when he let out an agonized yell.

Martine did the last few yards in double time. Ben was lying on the summit of the dune holding his foot, his face contorted with pain. Nearby was the cause of his distress— a thorn bush with vicious, curving thorns.

"Typical," he said through gritted teeth. "We walk for hours without seeing a single tree or blade of grass and the first bit of vegetation we come to is a thorn bush."

He let go of his foot and Martine saw five bleeding punctures on the sole. Before he could object, she'd unzipped her survival kit and was cleaning the tiny wounds with an antiseptic wipe. She followed it up with a dot or two of Grace's wound-healing potion, and wrapped his foot in gauze bandage to keep it sand-free while the *muti* did its work.

It was only when she'd finished and Ben was sitting up again and smiling that she noticed two things. The first was that there was a valley on the other side of the dune, spread with blond grass and a few trees. The other was that the thorn bush had yellow-green melons on it.

"Is that a mirage?" she said croakily.

"Is what a mirage?" Ben was examining Martine's handiwork, impressed at how professionally she'd patched him up. The potion she'd applied had reduced the pain to almost nothing.

Martine was examining the thorn bush. She tapped the forbidding cluster of thorns with her Swiss Army knife and several melons tumbled to the ground. She sliced one open. Inside it looked like a cucumber. She scooped out some of the yellow fruit and popped it into her mouth, grimacing slightly at its sour, burning taste. Next, she removed the shell from a couple of the seeds and ate the soft pellet inside.

"Martine, has the sun fried your brain?" demanded Ben. "Have you any idea how dangerous it is to eat unidentified plants? What if the fruit is poisonous? What if you get sick out here when we're miles from a doctor?"

Martine popped another few seeds into her mouth. "These are yummy. They're almost like almonds."

She cut open another melon and handed it to him. "This is a Nara bush. I'd recognize it anywhere. Grace is always going on about them. She says the San Bushmen love the Nara because it's the plant with a hundred uses. The oil from the seeds moisturizes the skin and protects it from sunburn; the root cures stomach pains, nausea, chest pains, and kidney problems; and the flesh can be rubbed on wounds to help heal them or eaten to rehydrate you."

Ben took a bit of convincing, but he was so starving and thirsty that he couldn't hold out for long, especially since Martine had dramatically revived since eating the first melon and was already tucking into the seeds of the second. Soon he was guzzling the seeds with equal enthusiasm.

At a certain point, they looked at each other, juice running down their chins, clothes and bodies filthy, hair sticking up on end from a night on the floor of the plane and a day in the baking desert, and burst out laughing.

It was almost dark by then, so they built a small fire with the dry twigs and foliage beneath the thorn bush and spread the thin blanket from the pilot's first aid box on top of the high narrow ridge of the dune. They covered themselves with the space blanket from Martine's survival kit, which could withstand temperatures of minus sixty degrees. Or so it claimed on the wrapper.

The evening star heralded the coming of the night.

Before long it was as if a box of diamonds had been spilled across the heavens, so numerous and glittering were the constellations. A crescent moon rose into the deep blue sky.

Ben and Martine lay with their heads resting on their packs, cozy beneath the space blanket, and gazed up at the Milky Way and Orion and the Southern Cross. From time to time, they heard the sounds of night creatures. It made them feel less alone.

"You know something, Ben?" Martine said sleepily. "I believe we're going to make it. I haven't a clue how, but I think we are."

Ben yawned. "You know something, Martine? I believe you're right."

They fell into the dreamless sleep of the young and the truly exhausted, innocent and, for the time being, uncaring, of what was to come.

14

They were woken by the rosy glow of dawn breaking over the red dunes. Ben sat up and declared the view to be the most breathtaking he'd ever seen. Martine, her voice thick with sleep, stayed where she was and moaned and groaned about the hardness of their sand bed and how freezing it was and how much she needed a shower and more sleep, as well as a breakfast of eggs, bacon, coffee, and orange juice.

"Coming right up, your ladyship. Just let me dial room service." Ben stood and pulled the blanket off her. "Get up, lazybones. I think you're going to want to see this." When she didn't stir, he aimed a gentle kick at her ribs.

Martine bolted upright and glared at him. "Boy, are you going to pay for that when we get back to civilization. Just you wait."

She shielded her eyes from the burning orange sun. "What's so special that I have to get out of bed at five a.m.?"

And then she saw them. In the valley below, scattered across the pale grass, were hundreds of Oryx antelope. They had extra-long horns, as straight and sharp as spears, and their coats and faces were patterned in fawn and black in such a way that they looked uniformed and regal, as if they formed part of some warrior queen's elite guard. Martine had only ever seen them in photos, but she'd always considered them to be among the world's most beautiful animals.

Tiredness forgotten, Martine jumped to her feet. "Ben, we have to go nearer. They're exquisite. A herd that size would need gallons of water to survive. Maybe we can see where they're getting it from."

Her change of heart made Ben smile, but he thought the better of teasing her. They packed up their things and slid down the dune. When they reached the valley they worked their way slowly toward the herd. Half an hour later, they were behind a tree and not far from a bare patch of earth where two young bulls were mock fighting. They tossed their magnificent heads and rushed at each other with their sword-like horns, turning aside at the last minute.

Martine couldn't bear the thought that they might harm each other. Ben had to restrain her from going to stop them.

"You shouldn't interfere with nature."

"Of course I'm going to interfere with nature if it means saving an Oryx from ending up stabbed and bleeding," Martine whispered. "Ouch, did you see that?"

The bulls clashed horns. The mock fighting was turning into real fighting.

Martine stepped from behind the tree. "Bad bulls!" she

cried. "Be nice to each other. What's the point of fighting?"

The bulls halted in their tracks. Their tails tossed as they pondered the apparition that had dared to intrude into their game. Then they galloped for the cover of the dunes, the herd stampeding after them.

"HEY!"

A young San Bushman rose seemingly from behind a tuft of grass. He was bare-chested and wearing khaki cargo shorts, and had a bow and sleeve of arrows slung over his shoulder and a professional-looking camera in his hand.

"I don't believe it," he said. "Thirteen thousand square miles of desert out here and you have to ruin my shot."

For much of the year she'd spent in Africa, Martine had been preoccupied with the San Bushmen. Accounts differed as to whether it was a Bushman legend or a Zulu legend or even just an African one that said that the child who rides a white giraffe will have power over all the animals. Regardless, it was the Bushmen, she felt sure, who held the key to her destiny.

Time and time again, their paintings had forecast the challenges she would have to face and overcome.

And yet in all these months it had never entered Martine's head that she might meet a San Bushman in the flesh. Certainly not one taking photographs with a long-lens camera. She'd always imagined them to be living in some remote region of the Kalahari Desert in Botswana or in the far north of Namibia, too nomadic and wedded to the traditions of their ancestors to be touched by the modern world.

But this boy, who looked to be about fifteen, was not enigmatic or far removed from the modern world. He was right here and quite angry.

"Do you know how long I've been lying here, waiting for that shot? I've had to put up with cold, with cramps, with ants nibbling my toes, and a scorpion crawling over my leg. At one point a horned adder even came to inspect me. I survive all that, only to have two idiot tourist kids come by and start shrieking at the Oryx as if they're pet donkeys."

"Look, I'm really, really sorry," said Martine. "How was I supposed to know I was interfering with your picture? I was only trying to stop the Oryx from goring each other. Anyway, you were camouflaged behind a blade of grass."

To her astonishment, the boy let out a shriek of delighted laughter. He clutched at his stomach and laughed some more.

Martine began to get annoyed. "What's so funny?"

"Camouflaged behind a blade of grass! I wish the elders of our tribe could hear you say that. They think I'm about the most useless hunter and tracker in San history. Which I probably am. Not that I care. All I ever wanted to be was a photographer, so I never bothered to learn any of that stuff. But then after my father . . . well, anyway now I wish I had, but it's too late."

"It's never too late," Ben assured him. "I'm an apprentice tracker. I could show you some stuff if you like."

This brought on another fit of laughter. "*You?* What do you track—the Yeti when it makes midnight visits to your school playing fields?"

He looked them up and down and Martine was conscious of what a sight they must be. "You're quite funny for tourist kids. And quite scruffy. Don't they have showers at your hotel? Where are all the other people on your tour anyway? I didn't hear an engine."

"We have a slight problem," confided Ben.

"A tiny one," Martine added supportively.

"Yesterday morning, we flew in on a private plane from the Western Cape in South Africa. We were with some . . . friends. They stopped at an airfield a few miles from here and Martine and I went to climb the dunes. They didn't realize we weren't on board and flew away without us."

The boy raised his eyebrows. "Your 'friends' didn't notice you were missing, even though there were only a handful of you on this plane?"

"That's right," Martine said brightly. "They probably got carried away taking pictures of the scenery. Like you!"

"Let me get this straight. You fly all the way from South Africa, stop at an airfield in the middle of the Namib Desert and decide to go off exploring on your own. Despite the dangers, nobody objects. While you're gone, your 'friends' abandon you in one-hundred-degree heat, with no food or water, and continue with their holiday as if nothing has happened?"

"It sounds worse than it is," said Martine.

"Oh, I think it's already pretty bad. With friends like that, who needs enemies?"

The boy looked at his watch. "All right, I'll take you to the police station in Swakopmond. It's about a six-hour drive from here, but lucky for you it's on my way. Good thing for you that you ruined my shot, hey?"

"We'd really appreciate a ride, but you don't need to go to the trouble of taking us to the police station," Ben put in quickly. "If you drop us in Swakopmond, we'll be fine. We'll make a few phone calls and have this sorted out in no time."

"Really?" said the boy. "I don't suppose there's anything you're not telling me, is there? You're not runaways or fugitives from the law, are you?"

Martine gave him her sweetest smile. "We're just ordinary kids having the worst vacation of our life."

"Right. If you say so." He took some keys from his pocket. "Let's go before it gets much hotter. My vehicle is parked behind those trees. Don't look so worried. I know I look about fifteen because I'm so small, but I've just turned eighteen and I do have my driver's license. I'm Gift, by the way."

"Gift," said Martine. "What a beautiful name."

A shadow passed across the boy's face. "It was my father's choice. I don't feel as if I've been much of a gift to him so far. Everything that's happened to him is entirely my fault. But that's another story. A long story. What are your names? Ben and Martine? All right, Ben and Martine, let's hit the road."

15

Once he'd recovered from the disappointment of missing out on his photo of the fighting Oryx, Gift was very friendly and chatty. Martine found it difficult to hide how in awe she was at being in the presence of a real San tribesman, even though he didn't fit her picture of a Bushman at all. Especially when he turned up the rap music on the sound system of his four-wheel drive.

It took a while for her to recover from her initial shyness, but after that she couldn't resist questioning him about the history of his tribe. He seemed surprised at her interest, but was more than willing to answer her. He told her how the San had been in southern Africa longer than any other indigenous people, and that their cave paintings dated back thousands of years.

For centuries they'd been skilled hunter-gatherers, living a nomadic life in harmony with nature. Then came the invaders. In the 1800s, white Afrikaaners moving in from South Africa and migrating Bantu tribes, who regarded the Bushmen as cattle thieves and lowlifes, brought so much pressure and conflict into the lives of the San that they were forced off their traditional lands and into the deserts of Botswana and Namibia. Their fragile, contented community began to crumble.

Many other things, such as the colonization of Namibia by Germany in the late nineteenth century, several wars, and the long struggle for independence, had contributed to destroying their way of life.

"Now we're scattered to the four winds and there are many social problems in our communities," Gift told Martine. "That's one of the reasons I went away to school. My father wanted me to have a better life than he and his father did. Instead that was the start of all the trouble."

He paused to slow his vehicle. It bucked and skidded as they descended into a rocky gorge. Martine hung out of the window, enjoying the coppery early-morning sunlight on her skin. The scenery had changed from red dunes to vast dry plains and hills ringed with terraces.

The colors of the landscape were extraordinary. Sometimes the soil was so white it glowed beneath the blue sky. Sometimes it was a warm brown and dotted with yellow flowers. Sometimes it was black and striped with mineral shades like purple, blue, and even green. They saw birds' nests as big as African huts with multiple entrances and yellow birds darting in and out. Gift explained that they were the home of the community weaverbird and could weigh as much a ton. Some were so heavy they brought down trees or branches.

"Why was going to school the start of all the trouble?" Ben asked Gift. "Didn't you want to go?"

Gift steered the four-wheel drive carefully along the

winding, rocky trail. "I very much wanted to go. My dream is to become a famous newspaper photographer. Because of that, I wanted to get the best education I could.

"The problems came when I went to high school in Windhoek. I had lots of cool friends and it made me see my family and old friends differently. When I'd return to our village in the holidays, everything looked so run-down and shabby. People, including my father, seemed ignorant; set in the past. They weren't part of the modern world at all. I had big fights with my father, Joseph. One night we argued after he told me he was unhappy with my attitude and was going to pull me out of school. I accused him of destroying my dream. I ran off into the desert. He came looking for me."

He stopped. Martine thought she saw a tear roll down his cheek, but he swerved to avoid a bounding springbok and when she looked again it was gone.

"Oh, forget it," Gift said roughly. "What's the point in me telling you this when I'm never going to see you again? And anyway, you're just two weird kids who've probably robbed a bank or something and are on the run."

"If we were on the run, we'd have chosen somewhere other than a scorching desert wilderness," Martine told him. "Look, we've still got a long way to travel. We might as well make conversation. What happened after you ran away into the desert? Did your father find you?"

Gift's strong brown hands gripped the wheel. "That's the terrible part. I came home the next morning, when I was hungry, to learn that my father had gone out searching for me. I felt sure he'd be back in a few hours. So did everyone else. But he never returned."

There was the briefest of pauses. "Not only did he not come back that day, he never came back at all. That was a year ago."

Martine stared at him in horror. "You mean, he just vanished without a trace?"

Gift focused on the road. "Without a trace. We sent our best trackers out to search for him and they didn't find so much as a footprint."

Martine's heart ached for him. It was bad enough when you did know what had happened to your parents. It had to be a thousand times worse having no idea.

"What did the police say?" Ben asked.

"They think he was eaten by some wild animal. They don't suspect foul play. My father was one of the most loved men in our tribe. He was an elephant whisperer."

"I've heard of horse whisperers," Ben said, "men and women who have a special gift for communicating with wild or traumatized horses. But what is an elephant whisperer? Surely you'd be trampled to death if you tried to whisper in the ear of a wild African elephant?"

Gift reached into his pocket and took out his wallet. He tossed it to Martine. "Show Ben the photo inside."

Martine slipped the photo out of its sleeve and she and Ben studied it. It showed a San Bushman like the ones she'd seen in books. He was standing between two elephants. The female elephant had her trunk curled around his waist, and he had one hand resting on her trunk and one on the tusk of a massive bull elephant. His face was radiant with happiness.

"Those are wild elephants."

Martine studied the picture again. "You mean, they're wild elephants that have been tamed?"

"No, they're totally wild. They'd gore you or me without blinking."

"But how is that possible?" Martine returned the photo to its sleeve and handed the wallet back to Gift.

He put it in his pocket. "When my father was four years old, the San camp was raided by desert elephants. There was a drought and they were looking for food. During the raid, he was snatched by one of the elephants. My grandparents assumed he'd been dragged away and killed, but three months later he was found alive and well and living quite happily with a herd of elephants. They rescued him with great difficulty, and were shocked to find he was reluctant to come home.

"Ever since, he has been able to communicate with elephants. Whether they know him or not, they seem to accept him as one of their own. Or, at least, they did before he disappeared. People think I'm out of my mind, but I believe that the elephants would not have allowed anything to happen to him. I'm positive that I will find him one day and he'll be living with elephants. I miss him so much."

"If it's any consolation, I know how you feel," Martine told him.

"No offense," Gift answered shortly, "but a kid like you couldn't possibly understand how I feel."

The car went quiet after that. They were passing a line of low, golden dunes that looked airbrushed and unreal, like a backdrop in a film set. Soon after that, they reached the little town of Swakopmond. Suddenly the sparkling sea was before them. Palm trees lined the beach.

The Germans had built Swakopmond during their occupation of Namibia, and the town looked a bit like a German film set. The architecture was German and the buildings spotlessly clean and prettily painted. The roads had names like Hendrik Witbool Street and Luderitz Street. Martine also spotted the Bismark Medical Center.

She nudged Ben. Leaning forward, he said, "Thanks for the ride, Gift. You've saved our lives. I don't know what we'd have done if you hadn't come along. We owe you. But we can manage on our own from now on. If you drop us somewhere around here, we'll find a phone and call our friends."

"Sure," responded Gift, but instead of pulling over he stamped hard on the accelerator. He swerved around another car, made a dangerous turn at the lights, and screeched to a halt in front of the police station.

Ben grabbed at the door handle, but it was locked.

"Sorry about that, but I couldn't afford to take any chances," Gift told him. "You seem like nice kids, but it's obvious you've told me a pack of lies about your so-called friends and their plane and their holiday. You've got thirty seconds to tell me the truth or I'm turning you in to the police."

16

A couple of lean, mean policemen, their hands resting casually on their gun belts strolled past the four-wheel drive. One of them turned as he passed and cast a suspicious eye over the vehicle and its passengers.

Martine's blood pressure went through the roof as she imagined her grandmother receiving a phone call in England to say that her granddaughter and Ben were in jail in Swakopmond, charged with stowing away on a private plane and entering Namibia illegally and without passports.

"You're right, Gift," she said. "We haven't been honest with you. We had a fight with our families and we ran away. We've learned our lesson, though, and we just want to call them, say sorry, and go home."

Gift opened the glove compartment and took out a cell phone. "What's the number? I'll dial it for you."

Martine swallowed. "I don't know it."

"You don't know your own phone number?"

He looked over at Ben. "How 'bout you?"

"There's nobody at my house. My parents are away on a cruise."

"Right, your thirty seconds are up. I'm getting the police and they can deal with you." He went to get out of the vehicle.

"Wait!" cried Martine. "I'm sorry. We'll tell you the real story."

Gift ignored her. He locked the doors from the outside and strode toward the police station.

"If I'd known I'd be spending my vacation in a Namibian jail, I might not have been so hasty about turning down the Mediterranean cruise," said Ben.

Martine banged hard on the window. "Gift," she yelled. "How would you feel if someone threatened to take away your home and everything and everyone you loved? Wouldn't you lie too? Wouldn't you do anything in your power to stop the people who wanted to do that?"

Two hours later, after a much-needed shower at Gift's aunt's house, the three of them were sitting in a restaurant called The Tug. It was an atmospheric place constructed from a tugboat that had been shipwrecked along the coastline—a stretch of ocean so treacherous that early explorers had named it the Skeleton Coast. Watching the Atlantic rollers charge up to the jetty outside and splatter the restaurant windows with gray foam, Martine was not in the least surprised.

"I want the whole truth and nothing but," said Gift as they tucked into prawns dripping with lemon and garlic, giant asparagus spears, and the biggest plate of fish and chips Martine and Ben had ever seen. "If you lie to me again, you'll be spending the next month washing dishes to pay for this meal."

So they told him the whole story. Well, almost the whole story. Martine explained about the fire that had killed her parents, and about moving to Africa. She decided against telling him about Grace's prediction. It seemed pointless when she had no idea what it meant.

Gift heard her out, his face filled with compassion. "I'm sorry for saying that a kid like you could never understand what I've been through. Obviously you do."

Ben took up the story. He told Gift about the sinister businessman who'd shown up out of the blue one day, claiming that Henry Thomas had signed over Sawubona to him as surety for a debt and giving them less than a fortnight to leave the reserve. He and Martine were, he said, so determined to save Sawubona that coming to Namibia to investigate the man who wanted to take every-thing from them had seemed their only option.

"Do you know where he has his business?" asked Gift.

"No," admitted Martine. "We think he might own some tourist lodges, but we're not really sure. A few years ago, he gave my grandfather a desert elephant from Damaraland. She was very badly injured, and we have a sanctuary that helps heal wild animals that have been wounded or mistreated. He said she came from a zoo that had shut down."

Gift frowned. "That's odd. I myself am from Damar-aland. That's where my father disappeared. We don't have zoos in Namibia, and if one had opened or closed down in our area I'd definitely know about it, because my father has records about practically every elephant in the desert.

"The other thing that puzzles me is why this man would send an injured elephant out of the country. We have plenty of wildlife hospitals and sanctuaries of our own. It makes no sense at all."

He paused to shovel in a mouthful of fish. "He sounds like a thoroughly evil character. What's his name? Maybe I've heard of him."

"His name is James," Ben told him. "Reuben James."

Gift choked. His fish went down the wrong way, and he had such a severe coughing fit that he needed almost a whole bottle of water to recover. It was some time before he could speak again.

"That's impossible," he croaked, eyes streaming.

Martine was bewildered. "Why is it impossible?"

Gift took another swallow of water. "Because the man you're describing sounds like a nasty, heartless piece of work. I've known Reuben James since I was a boy, and he is the opposite of that. He's a conservationist. He's poured a fortune of his own money into protecting the desert elephants. When my father disappeared, it was Reuben James who organized all the patrols that went out searching for him. He's the man who paid for my education and he helped me get a job as a freelance photographer for a local magazine.

"Reuben James is the best man I know."

17

It was Angel who saved the day.

Sitting on Swapokmond beach early the next morning, drinking coffee and tucking into a slab of Black Forest cake from Anton's famous German bakery, Martine thought there was something ironic about the fact that the elephant, who'd been intent on hurting them at Sawubona, had indirectly ended up helping them in Namibia. But then maybe Ben was right. Maybe she'd only ever intended to harm Lurk. And that raised a lot of questions.

The way it happened was this. Gift had taken the news about Reuben James badly, to say the least. He'd been ready to cart them back to the police station just for criticizing the man. Even when Martine pointed out that he himself had described Reuben as a "thoroughly evil character" before he knew who they were talking about, he was still reluctant to accept that his mentor could be flawed.

But then Ben recounted the conversation they'd overheard on the plane, and Martine followed it up by telling Gift about Angel's attack on the chauffeur.

When he heard about Lurk, the stubborn scowl left the

San boy's face. He sat up straight. "Are you telling me that this desert elephant—the elephant given to your grandfather by Reuben James—singled out Lurk and charged him?"

"Apparently," said Martine. "And when Lurk escaped by throwing down his jacket, she mashed it into the earth as if she hated it."

Gift nodded. "I know how she feels. Lurk is sly. Cunning. Whenever Reuben James is around, he's all smiles and politeness and yes sir, no sir. The minute Reuben is out of sight, he's an arrogant brute. He'll kick a dog as soon as look as it, and he's forever making spiteful comments about the San people and hinting that we're all cattle thieves and drunkards. No one understands why Reuben has him around.

"What's interesting is that your elephant Angel seems to have remembered him years after she left Namibia. That almost certainly means he's done something cruel to her in the past. For that reason alone, I'm prepared to help you. As for what you overheard on the plane, I'm sure there's an innocent explanation. I can't believe Reuben is mixed up in anything dodgy."

Martine and Ben, who were by then so exhausted that their eyes were closing at the dinner table, were too grateful to him for feeding them and agreeing to assist them to argue. They were also thankful to him for providing them with shelter. Gift's aunt hadn't minded in the least allowing two young strangers to sleep on her floor for a night, especially since they were leaving before breakfast. She'd even done their laundry.

Sitting on the beach, Martine popped the last choco-latey morsel of cake into her mouth and checked the time. It was six a.m. After depositing them at Anton's café with a handful of money and instructions to pick up supplies and meet him near The Tug restaurant, Gift had gone to get fuel and water. They had another long drive ahead of them.

An early-morning sea fog hovered over Swakopmond, and the ocean looked gray and wintry. The palm trees creaked and sighed. Martine huddled closer to Ben for warmth. They shared the last of her coffee.

"Have you noticed," she asked him, "how everything keeps coming back to Angel? It's almost as if the key to understanding what Reuben James is up to and why he's trying to get his hands on Sawubona is the elephant. If we can get to the bottom of her story, of why he gave her to my grandfather in the first place, we might uncover his secret."

Ben handed her back the coffee cup. "That's funny, I just had the exact same thought. The thread that runs through everything is the elephant's tale."

Gift materialized behind them. He had a disconcerting habit of appearing out of nowhere. "What elephant's tail?"

"They're cute," said Martine, "elephant's tails."

Gift jiggled his keys. "I suppose they are. Come on, we need to hit the road. I can't wait to get home to Dama-raland."

The drive north was not nearly as interesting as the one to Swakopmond, but it had a bleak appeal nonetheless. For the first hour they followed the Skeleton Coast, still shrouded in sea fog. Martine found her mood lifted as soon as they turned inland and left behind the gloomy cloud.

There followed three hours of flat, rocky desert, interrupted only by the occasional gaily decorated house, or neat roadside stall selling chunks of shimmering pink quartz and leopard stone. They stopped at one, and Martine was sure she could feel a kind of warm energy coming off a piece of pink quartz when she lifted it.

Gift gave the rock seller a crate of water. In the desert, he told them, people shared what they could. The man was from the Herero tribe and had buttery brown skin enhanced by many bracelets and other trinkets. He summoned his wife from their thatched house and Martine's mouth dropped open when the woman emerged, followed by three small children. She was magnificently dressed in a colorful outfit styled in the manner of a Victorian missionary. A bright yellow banana-shaped hat sat lengthways across her head.

She explained to Martine and Ben that Herero women had worn the dresses for centuries and that they were a symbol of great pride.

Martine felt very self-conscious in her ragged jeans and old T-shirt. She cast a look around the barren landscape, simmering under the harsh desert sun, and couldn't imagine where the Herero mother found the energy, or the water, to look that good.

"We have only ourselves to blame if our country is desert," the rock seller told her, reading her thoughts. He nodded at Gift. "If he is from the San tribe, he can probably tell you why."

"There is a Bushman legend about the lack of water in Namibia," Gift explained to Ben and Martine. "It's said that many moons ago, our ancestors were very poor. They complained bitterly about how hard their lives were. They thought of little else. They prayed and wished that they could be rich. They were sure that if they could only be wealthy, their lives would be perfect. So God granted their wish. He crystallized all the rivers and lakes in Namibia and turned them into diamonds."

"Now we have many diamonds and other precious minerals like platinum," said the rock seller. "Namibia is one of the richest countries in Africa. But we have nothing to drink."

He thanked them again for the water and they continued on their way. A range of violet mountains appeared on the horizon. The desert gave way to grassland and then they climbed the mountains and dropped over the other side. Martine could not get over how the road ahead just seemed to stretch on forever, into infinity. Above them, the sky bubbled with clouds that changed by the second, like some dizzying kaleidoscope.

Early in the afternoon, Gift pointed at a distant hill of massive boulders, a bit like those Martine and Ben had come across in the Matopos in Zimbabwe, and said proudly: "There's my house."

The two friends exchanged glances. Even after they'd unloaded the supplies from the vehicle and followed Gift up the steep path between the rocks, they still couldn't see any sign of habitation. Then they rounded a boulder and there, perched on the edge of the hill and overlooking a lovely, tranquil valley, were three thatched domes. Beneath the domes were two-bedroom tents with showers at the rear, and one living room tent with a splash pool cut into the deck in front of it.

Gift grinned at their expressions. "This land has been in our family for generations and my father always talked of building a house here. When I started working at the magazine, I saved every cent I made and put it toward creating this place. Reuben James was kind enough to arrange for some of his hotel workers to help me thatch the domes and put up the tents. There have been many challenges, such as drilling a borehole to get water, but it has been worth it. This is my father's favorite valley, because it is the gathering place of many desert elephants. When he returns, I want him to have a special place to come home to."

Gazing around the tents, which were simply but lovingly furnished in African cotton and wood, Martine felt tears spring to her eyes. Gift's father had gone missing in one of the most treacherous desert environments on the planet, and yet his son had never given up hope they would be reunited. He still talked of his dad in the present tense, as if he might round the corner at any time.

That evening, she sat with Ben and Gift on a high, flat

boulder, watching the setting sun sink behind the mountains. As the rocks glowed orange, the clouds became lacy wisps of pink, and the contours of the valley became a carpet of jade-colored velvet, she thought again of the San boy's courage. It inspired her to keep faith that, against all odds, she'd see Jemmy and her grandmother again.

When Gift moved away to stoke the barbecue, sending sparks flying, Ben said simply, "From tomorrow, it'll be five days."

Martine knew exactly what he meant. There were five days until Christmas Eve, the deadline for saving Sawubona and the date Gwyn Thomas was due to return from London. Five days for them to investigate Reuben James's business dealings and get to the bottom of the mystery surrounding Angel; five days to unravel Grace's prophecy; and five days for them to figure out how to travel thousands of miles back to Storm Crossing without money, transport, or passports.

They turned at the same moment to look at Gift. The San boy had his back to them and was loading pieces of chicken onto the sizzling grill. Martine's stomach did an uncomfortable flip, as if she were in an elevator that was descending too quickly. They had less than a week to achieve a minor miracle and they were utterly dependent on a stranger—one who owed his home and his job to the man they were investigating.

18

Gift's home was so peaceful and magical that, as she lay in bed the next morning watching the sun outline the hills with gold and drinking the campfire-brewed coffee Ben had brought her, Martine fantasized about one day owning a tented camp overlooking an African valley herself. The dream lasted only until she nearly contracted hypothermia trying to have an outdoor shower using a bucket of icy water. After that, she vowed to stay in her grandmother's comfortable thatched house at Sawubona, with its hot running water, for the rest of her days.

That's not going to happen unless you can outwit Reuben James, piped up a voice in her head, but she refused to listen to it. It was too beautiful a morning to dwell on the disaster looming back in South Africa.

Breakfast (two fried eggs on toast) out of the way, they went in search of the famous desert elephants, which Martine and Ben were dying to see. Gift had warned them not to get their hopes up. Despite the creatures' immense size they were frequently difficult to find, because their daily searches for food and water meant they traveled enormous distances.

"That's one of the reasons it's so hard to keep an accurate count of their numbers," said Gift, braking to allow a herd of springbok to cross the road. "Before my father disappeared he'd become concerned about the way elephants kept vanishing, supposedly without any cause. These were not sick or old elephants. They were from herds he'd followed for years, so there wasn't any doubt about what was happening. Young, healthy animals would just go missing from the herd. One day he'd see them, the next they'd be gone."

Kind of like the elephant whisperer himself, thought Martine. She wound down her window and stared out at the blur of flaxen grasses and twisting red road and far-off violet mountains. The African landscape was so enchanting it was hard to believe that tragedy, in the form of poisonous snakes, plants, scorpions, savage beasts, and even the merciless sun, stalked it.

"My father alerted the authorities," Gift went on, his eyes skimming the trees for any sign of elephants, "but nobody took him seriously apart from Reuben James, who increased the poaching patrols. People kept telling Pa that these elephants must have died of starvation or thirst and that the other members of the herd were burying them in an elephants' graveyard."

"The elephants have a cemetery?" Ben said in amazement.

Gift snorted. "No, that's just a tourist myth, but they do hold elephant funerals. Sometimes they'll lift up the body of a companion, a bit like human mourners will reverently carry a coffin, and they bury their dead by covering them with mud or leaves and branches. Anyway, in the end it was decided that global warming was killing the elephants."

"Global warming?" Martine was puzzled. "You mean how the earth's surface is heating up because we're polluting the planet so much with our cars, airplanes, and factories? What's that got to do with disappearing elephants?"

"Scientists and politicians always seem to be arguing about whether or not global warming exists," Ben said.

"You can't take any notice of politicians because they're just trying to get elected," Gift told him. "It's true that some scientists claim it doesn't exist, but most agree that the warming of the earth's surface is going to lead to sea level rises, the melting of the polar ice caps, and an increase in disease and extreme weather."

"And if there's an increase in extreme weather, the drought periods in Namibia will be worse than ever and the desert elephants will be pushed to the brink of extinction?" guessed Martine.

"Exactly. We're already witnessing that now. Except that my father didn't feel it was lack of food and water that was causing these elephants to go missing. To him, it seemed too targeted. It was always the prime specimens from every herd that went missing. And yet there was no evidence of poaching."

"It's almost as if you have a Bermuda Triangle here in Damaraland," remarked Ben.

"What's a Bermuda Triangle?" asked Martine.

"*The* Bermuda Triangle is this area of the Florida Straits, the Bahamas, and the Caribbean where loads of aircraft and ships have gone missing and have never been seen or heard from again. It's almost as if they've been swallowed by the ocean. Over the years, hundreds of experts on things like weather and paranormal activity have tried to discover what became of them, but a lot of the vanishings are completely unexplained."

"I don't know about that," said Gift, "but I'm convinced the two things are linked. You know, my father going missing and the disappearing elephants. The funny thing is no elephants have been lost since the day my father vanished."

Ben said excitedly: "Gift, back up and check out that tree. I'm sure I saw some fresh elephant sign."

Gift carried on driving. As much as he liked Ben and Martine, he continued to view them as tourist kids who knew nothing about the desert. "Leave the tracking to me, city boy," he said jokingly. "The elephants never come this far south."

Martine smiled to herself. In the few months Ben had been studying under Tendai as an apprentice tracker, he'd shown such a talent for reading sign, the tracker's word for the traces an animal leaves of its passing, that the game warden said he had the potential to become one of the best he'd ever seen.

Two hours later, her smile had gone and her patience had evaporated. It was clear that Gift was as poor at tracking as he'd joked he was when he met them. They hadn't seen so much as a tail-hair of an elephant.

Gift read her expression and scowled. "If you and Ben think you can do better, *you* find the elephants."

Ben said nothing. He sat staring straight ahead while Gift grudgingly drove back to the tree where he'd first spotted the peeled bark and split branches that so often marked the passage of elephants. When they reached it, Ben hopped out and inspected the elephant tracks at close range. Martine pored over them with him. She could never get over the fact that a beast weighing up to seven tons could leave such a light impression on the earth. They seemed to move as lightly as dancers.

"That way," Ben said with quiet authority, pointing across a dry riverbed.

Gift did as he was instructed, although his face said: "Yeah, right." But his disbelief turned to awe as Ben moved rapidly from sign to sign. By the time they crested a rise to find the desert elephants browsing in the trees before them, Martine could see that Gift had gained a new respect for her friend. Not that he admitted it. He said, "I was planning to check this place next anyway."

The bull elephant separated himself from the herd gathered in the shade of a thicket of trees and advanced up the dusty trail, his ears flapping warningly. The females, the matriarchs, gathered their youngsters in close.

And now it was Gift's chance to shine, because if there was one thing the San boy did know about, it was elephant behavior. His father had taught him everything he knew.

"A herd of elephants is like a moving nursery and retirement village for the elderly," he told them with a laugh as he parked a respectful distance away and turned the engine off. "It's a real community with everyone looking out for each other. They know every fellow member by what we call a name, and they can use a sort of elephant sonar to find friends who are as far as six miles away."

"Tendai says that their pregnancy lasts two years," Ben said.

Martine gazed out of the window at the huge beasts. "That's got to be mighty uncomfortable, especially when you think how big the elephant baby would be."

Gift smiled. "Yes, but elephants get a lot more support than a lot of humans do. An elephant baby is born into a protective circle, with a midwife standing by, and all share in the caring of it, including the feeding."

"Dolphins do the same thing," Martine said excitedly. "A dolphin midwife will even assist the newborn to the surface of the water for its first breath."

She looked at Ben. Both were remembering the days they'd spent swimming with dolphins in the islands of Mozambique on another adventure.

Watching the ponderous progress of an old matriarch, Ben said with a laugh, "If an elephant tried swimming, it would sink to the bottom of the lake."

"Actually," Gift told him, "apart from whales and dolphins, elephants are the best swimmers in the whole mammal kingdom. They've been known to swim up to three hundred miles between islands—just for fun."

At Sawubona, Martine had always regarded elephants as lumbering, prehistoric-looking creatures that were wondrous but unfathomable. Their activities appeared to be confined to eating trees and splashing around the water hole. Gift showed her that even their tiniest action had significance.

"See that youngster over there? He's using that stick as a fly switch. Elephants have complex brains and an incredible ability to reason, and they're masters at using tools to make tasks easier. They use chewed-up bark to plug holes in riverbeds so that the water doesn't evaporate and they can return to drink later. They uproot trees and push them onto electric fences. There've been stories of them pretending to be chained after they've broken their shackles so they can escape from their captors or take revenge against people who've been cruel to them."

Martine thought again of Angel and wondered who, or what, had traumatized her in the past.

"Funny," said Ben, "whenever I see an animal that's cute and cuddly and small, like a Labrador puppy, or big and gentle, like dolphins or Martine's giraffe, Jemmy, all I want to do it protect it and make sure nothing ever hurts it. But elephants look like they can take care of themselves. They're so big and their hides are so thick that it's never occurred to me they might be able to reason like we do or have similar emotions."

"Hunters like to believe that when animals are killed they don't know what's happening to them, but elephants feel things every bit as strongly as we feel them," Gift assured him. "They have all the same emotions: love, hate, rage, pride, happiness, jealousy, and despair. Baby elephants who've witnessed their parents being culled wake up screaming with nightmares."

Martine, who'd endured many nightmares after her own parents died, regarded the elephants with new eyes. She'd taken those at Sawubona for granted. Although she saw these sensitive, intelligent beasts almost every day, she knew next to nothing about them. Well, that was going to change. She was going to do what she could to make their lives better, and the elephant she was going to start with was Angel.

They were driving back across the plain, their senses full of the majesty of the elephants, when Gift spotted a Velvetchia plant. It was, he said, the oldest in the world and they absolutely had to see it. Some were known to live for thousands of years.

Martine, who was conscious of time slipping away from them like salt through a timer, was too distracted to take much interest in the plant, which was quite ugly. The calls of a pair of sandgrouse birds attracted her attention and she wandered over to them. That's when she noticed the circle of red earth. At its widest point it was probably the length Jemmy would be if he lay down, and it was perfectly round and bare. Not a blade of grass grew on it.

She touched it gingerly. The ground was firm and the soil was warm and crumbly. When she sifted it through her fingers, nothing happened. There was no blinding flash of light. No life-changing revelation.

"Gift," she called. "Do you know anything about this circle?"

He came over. "Sure I do. That's a fairy circle."

"A *fairy* circle? You believe in fairies in Namibia?"

Gift laughed. "I don't think anyone believes they're created by actual fairies. Then again, nobody knows where they come from. They appear out of nowhere, a bit like crop circles do in places like Britain and America. Some people think they're caused by termites or radioactive granite; others say a forest of Euphorbia trees grew here many years ago and poisoned the ground when they died."

"What do you believe?" Ben asked.

"I think they were made by little green aliens," Gift teased. "They're extra-terrestrial landing pads!"

"You keep saying 'they,'" Martine interrupted. "Is there another circle around here?"

Gift clutched at his forehead, as if that was the dumbest tourist question he'd heard. Motioning them to follow, he clambered up a rocky hillock. When they reached the top, sweating from the short climb, he waved an arm in the direction of the grassy plain on the other side. Martine peered over the edge and gulped. As far as the eye could see were dozens and dozens of circles.

The circle will lead you to the elephants, Grace had told her.

"Which circle?" Martine thought in despair. And which elephants? If Grace was right, only one combination would lead her to the truth.

19

The next step in their investigation was Reuben James's tourist lodge. Gift was friends with one of the guides there and he thought it possible the man might know something about Angel's past. He was less willing to cooperate when it came to the lodge owner himself. "You're wasting your time doing detective work on Reuben James," he told them. "There's nothing to find. But, hey, it's your vacation."

Martine said nothing on the drive over. She'd not yet recovered from the fairy circle blow. She'd expected to find one special circle that would make everything clear, not hundreds. Once again she was haunted by the notion that she and Ben might be in the wrong place at the wrong time. That by coming to Namibia in the vain hope of stumbling upon some last-ditch way of saving Sawubona and the animals, they might have ruined any chance Gwyn Thomas had of doing just that.

She shuddered to think what would happen if her grand-mother arrived back at the game reserve unexpectedly to learn that not only had her granddaughter and Ben been missing for days, the police had not been called. She'd go berserk. She'd feel obliged to get a message to Ben's mum and dad on their Mediterranean cruise and all hell would break loose. Grace, who'd promised to take care of Martine and Ben, would be in the biggest trouble of her life. So would Tendai, who was skeptical about Grace's prophesies and would have been livid to discover that the *sangoma* had encouraged Martine to go off on some hare-brained adventure "to pluck out the thorn" that was hurting her.

Then there was the problem of the prophecy itself. Grace's predictions were often obscure, but this latest one was either deceptively simple or just plain wrong. The circle hadn't led Martine to the elephants. The elephants had, if anything, led her to the circle.

On top of all that, she was worried sick about Jemmy and Khan. Sawubona was crawling with Reuben James's hired workers. What if one took a shine to the white giraffe and rare leopard and decided to steal them?

Gift's voice broke into her thoughts. "Welcome to Hoodia Haven."

Martine leaned out the window. They were pulling into a circular gravel driveway lined with beds of cacti and purple and scarlet desert flowers, shaped to spell the name of the lodge.

"That's a strange name for a hotel," Ben remarked.

"I think it's quite a good one," Gift said, parking beneath a shepherd's tree. They all climbed out. "Those plump cacti are hoodia plants. The iKung Bushmen call them *'xhoba.'* For thousands of years the San have used them as appetite suppressants and thirst quenchers. A piece the size of a cucumber used to keep the old hunters going for a week."

"That would be handy right now," remarked Martine. "It seems at least a century since we ate breakfast."

Gift took a knife from his pocket and cut them each a piece of cactus, using a rag to protect his hands from the thorns. "When you've eaten that, why don't you go and wait in the guest lounge? There's an exhibition of my elephant photos in there. I'll go and ask my friend about your elephant."

Ben waited until he was out of earshot. "What's our plan?" he asked, screwing up his nose at the bitterness of the cactus leaf, then straightening it again as he realized that it left a refreshing sweet taste on his tongue. "What exactly are we searching for?"

"We don't know," admitted Martine, wiping her hands on a tea-tree wipe Gift had provided. "Some proof that Mr. James is involved in diamond smuggling or mistreats animals or is employing slave labor or something. Proof of corruption. Why don't we split up and see if we can find anything interesting?"

"Sounds good. Martine . . ."

"Yes?"

"Watch your back."

Martine did not have much experience with five-star hotels, but there was no doubt that Hoodia Haven was the last word in luxury. The swimming pool looked as if it had been created from dissolved aquamarines. Over-tanned guests were draped around it in elegant poses, ice tinkling in their drinks. One had binoculars and was watching zebra drink from a distant water hole. Waiters glided around with platters of fruit, shellfish, and salad, or whisked away empty cocktail glasses with umbrellas sticking out of them.

The hoodia plant had taken the edge off Martine's hunger, but the food looked so delicious it was hard not to want it. When she passed an unattended bowl of exotic fruit and nuts, she sneaked a handful of salted almonds into her mouth. A waiter noticed and smiled. A few minutes later he came over and kindly presented her with a plate of chopped pineapple.

Martine kept expecting to be outed as an imposter and evicted, but nobody took any notice of her. She sat nibbling the pineapple, which tasted and smelled like nectar. When she'd finished it, she thanked the waiter and set off along a corridor marked "Spa" and "Gift Shop."

With every step, her hopes of finding a clue that might save Sawubona evaporated. Everything about the lodge appeared eco-friendly and aboveboard. The staff had warm smiles and were going about their work contentedly. The guests were in a state of bliss. There could hardly have been a place in Namibia that looked less like a den of corruption.

She rounded a corner and there was Reuben James. He was strolling toward her, but he was focused on his companion, who was speaking.

Martine wanted to move, but her limbs felt heavy and useless, and her brain functioned at half speed, as if its batteries were almost flat. At the last conceivable moment, she bounded sideways into the gift shop.

From a small office at the back of the store, a disembodied voice called: "I'll be with you as soon as I can, honey. I'm just finishing up an order. If you want to try anything on, the changing room is free. I'm Theresa. Give me a yell if you need help."

"Thanks, Theresa, I will," said Martine.

She snatched a couple of T-shirts off a shelf and shot into the changing room just as Reuben James came into view. Soon afterward, she heard his voice raised in cheerful greeting outside in the parking lot. She stood on the cubicle stool and peered through the slits in the air vent. Reuben had his hand on Gift's shoulder and was congratulating him on his exhibition of photographs. Gift was smiling.

When Gift moved away, Reuben's companion, who was in shadow and could only partially be seen from Martine's angle, said, "You genuinely care for that boy, don't you? How can you look him in the eye?"

"Easily," Reuben James responded shortly. "First, because what he doesn't know isn't going to hurt him. Second, because very soon I'm going to put everything right. And lastly, because I'm thinking about the bigger picture. What I'm doing is for the good of everyone in Namibia."

"Oh, sure," drawled his companion. "You're all heart."

"Look around you," Reuben James said heatedly. "Can you not see that global warming is a devastating threat to the already impossibly hard lives of the desert tribes and animals here?"

Martine was startled to hear global warming mentioned twice in one morning. She strained her ears, trying not to miss a word.

Reuben James went on: "Can't you see that the Ark Project is going to transform the lives of thousands, including that of the boy?"

"I can see how it's going to transform your bank balance."

"And yours."

"To be sure," said the stranger. He moved slightly, revealing the back of his head and his broad shoulders. His hair had the shiny blue-blackness of a crow's wing. "But then I'm not pretending I'm going to save the planet."

He cocked his glossy black head and studied the other man. "What I want to know is, are you prepared for the catastrophic effect that this is going to have? Are you prepared for *war?*"

Reuben James rounded on him angrily. "What are you talking about, Callum? There's not going to be a war."

"Are you sure about that? Can you say that for certain? And anyway, I thought you told me you were prepared to do whatever it took. I wouldn't like to think that you were going soft on me at the eleventh hour. I might have to take drastic measures. I might have to, say, call in that loan."

Reuben James looked at him with contempt. "I meant

what I said. I *will* do whatever it takes. But when this is over, I don't ever want to lay eyes on you again." And with that he climbed into a sleek silver car and sped away in a plume of dust.

The stranger watched him go. "Don't worry," he said so softly that Martine barely caught the words. "You won't."

As if some instinct told him he was being observed, he whipped around and stared straight at the vent.

Martine leaped clumsily off the stool, knocking it over in her haste.

"Is everything okay in there?" called Theresa.

To buy herself time, Martine called, "These T-shirts are lovely, but I need a smaller size."

A cocoa-brown hand with red-painted nails slipped around the curtain and took them from her. "I should say so, honey. These are men's extra-large. They'd look like dresses on you. I'll nip out to the storeroom and see if we've got them in kids' sizes."

The gift shop fell silent. Martine's head was spinning. *Are you prepared for war?* That was the sentence that kept going through her mind over and over. She had to talk to Ben. If she was quick, she could get out to the parking lot before Theresa returned. She pulled back the curtain.

Standing at the shop counter, half turned away from her but looking every bit as surly as he had when she last saw him at Sawubona, was Lurk.

20

The brass rings screeched as Martine wrenched shut the curtain. Had he seen her or hadn't he? She thought he might have, but she couldn't be sure.

The seconds stretched into minutes. The gift shop stayed silent. Martine stood pressed up against the back wall of the cubicle, praying for Theresa's return. She seemed to have been gone forever. Then she heard footsteps—not the saleswoman's clicking heels, but the heavy, deliberate tread of a man's shoe. They came around the counter and stopped outside the changing room.

Martine's heart almost stopped with them. She could hear Lurk breathing. He slid back the curtain.

Martine screamed.

A henna-haired Damara woman she took to be Theresa came rushing in, followed by Gift. Martine caught a glimpse of Ben close on their heels, but he spotted the chauffeur in the nick of time and took rapid evasive action.

"Lurk, have you lost your mind? What do you mean by terrorizing my customers?" the saleswoman demanded.

"Yes, Lurk, have you lost your mind?" parroted Gift,

unable to resist the opportunity to make fun of the man he loathed.

The chauffeur glowered at him. "I know this girl," he told Theresa, pointing rudely at Martine. "She from South Africa. Very bad witch. She make buffalo rise from the dead and the elephant to chase me."

Theresa went red with annoyance. "What rubbish are you talking, Lurk? As if a young girl could resurrect buffaloes and order elephants to charge you. Have you been drinking?"

"I *know* her," Lurk insisted. "She ride white giraffe."

"Don't be ridiculous, Lurk," said Gift. "This is Anna, the sister of a friend of mine from Windhoek. She's staying at the lodge with her family."

Lurk's bulging eyes seemed to bulge even more. His chin rose defiantly. "Not Anna. She Maxine. No, no, *Martine*. She from South Africa; from Mr. James's new safari park."

"Lurk, you've just heard Gift say that this girl is a friend of his from Windhoek," snapped Theresa, beginning to lose her temper. "She is also a guest of Mr. James at this hotel and the notion that she's some kind of animal magician, riding giraffes and ordering lions and elephants about, is absolutely preposterous. Now, if you want to remain in Mr. James's employment another day, my strong suggestion is that you apologize to this young lady, pull yourself together, and get back to work."

"Sorry for mistake," growled Lurk, not looking in the least bit contrite. As he slouched from the gift shop,

Martine heard him mumble: "Very bad witch, I no forget this."

"Please accept my sincerest apologies, Anna," Theresa said, embarrassed. "I can't think what's got into him. He can be a bit odd at times, but today he seems quite deranged."

"No problem at all," Martine assured her, anxious to get away in case Reuben James came to investigate the disturbance. "It's an easy mistake to make. He obviously has a grudge against this girl Maxine."

"*Mar*tine," Gift corrected helpfully.

"Let me make it up to you, honey," Theresa offered. "Is there anything you'd like? Can I give you a Hoodia Haven T-shirt?"

"Really, it's not necessary," said Martine, feeling like a fraud. The last thing she wanted was a T-shirt advertising her archenemy's hotel.

But Theresa was adamant she take something, so Martine reluctantly accepted a piece of rose quartz the saleswoman was using as a paperweight. It wasn't for sale, she told Martine. It was just some rock she'd picked up by the roadside.

Martine suspected that it was worth far more than Theresa made out, but she couldn't refuse without seeming ungrateful. It could be a present for her grandmother if she ever saw her again. *When,* Martine told herself firmly. *When* she saw her grandmother again.

Thanking Theresa profusely, she and Gift left the shop. As soon as they were in the corridor, Gift said in a low voice, "That was a close call. I think we'd better go before you get yourself into any more trouble. You round up Ben. I need to check with reception to see if the camera lens I've ordered has arrived."

He strode away across the courtyard. Ben stepped out from behind a potted palm tree.

"Ben, did you see what happened?" cried Martine. "Lurk recognized me. He came after me like a psycho."

"Never mind about that now," said Ben. "I've got something to show you and I don't want Gift to know about it just yet."

Ordinarily Martine would have been hurt by his lack of concern, but she could see at once he was onto something. His face was alight with it.

Keeping an eye out for Lurk, who was sure to be as cross as a snake after the gift shop humiliation, he led Martine to the guest lounge, where Gift's elephant exhibition had been hung. Three women were sitting in the corner tucking into tea and sponge cake, but they were deep in conversation and barely glanced up.

The photos were of a herd of elephants. They were taken over the course of a single day, starting with the first ray of dawn and ending with the ascent of the evening star. Gift had arranged them in a panorama around the room. The rich and varied life of the herd, and the spirit of individual elephants, shone from them.

"Ben, they're wonderful, but are you sure we have time for this?"

Ben gestured toward three photographs taken shortly

before sunset and said, "This won't take long. What do you notice about these pictures?"

Martine found it difficult to concentrate after the scene in the gift shop. "Umm, I don't know. I guess they're well composed."

"Do you see anything unusual about the elephants?"

"They look like a normal herd of elephants to me. Ben, we should go."

Ben said patiently, "Look closely. There are sixteen elephants in the first and second picture and fifteen in the third."

"So what?" Martine checked the door, half expecting Lurk to burst through it. "The pictures were taken five or ten minutes apart. Maybe one of the elephants sloped off to devour a tree."

"Could be. Only the missing elephant is a young bull. He's walking slightly apart from the others in the first and second picture. He's in the background. That's why you don't notice him if you only glance at the photos. In the third picture, he's not there anymore and the other elephants seem to be milling around as if they're fretting or distressed."

He paused. "Now look again at the second picture and see what's in his path."

Martine squinted at the photo. "A fairy circle!"

"I think," said Ben, "we've just found our Bermuda Triangle."

21

"The Ark Project?" repeated Gift. "Those were Reuben James's words?"

"I think so," said Martine. After questioning Gift and learning that the elephant photographs had been taken on the plain near the Stone Age rock engravings in Twyfelfontein, she'd asked if they could visit them.

"I was listening through a vent," she went on, "but I'm fairly sure that's what he called it. He talked about global warming and how what he was doing was for the good of everyone in Namibia."

"What did I tell you?" said Gift. "You're both so ready to believe he's a fraudster because you're upset he's bought your game reserve, but what you overheard proves that he's a generous, decent man. The Ark Project sounds like some sort of conservation scheme, or maybe it's a code name for the new hotel he's building."

"Sounds like a Doomsday project to me," murmured Ben.

Martine was getting heartily sick of Gift defending his mentor. "They don't prove anything. For starters, he hasn't bought Sawubona, he's tricked my grandfather into signing it away . . ."

"You don't know that."

". . . and besides, the man who was with him, the one with blue-black hair like crow's feathers—"

"I've never seen him before."

"Well, he accused your Mr. James of pretending to save the planet only because he wanted to make himself richer."

Gift slowed the vehicle and turned down a gravel track leading to a ring of rocky mountains. "That doesn't prove anything either. Reuben's a businessman. Of course he has to work out if a project makes financial sense."

Martine could have easily burst his bubble by telling him how Reuben James had told Callum that what Gift didn't know "can't hurt him," and that he planned to "put things right." She could have told him that the men were planning to start a "war." But she couldn't bring herself to do that—not yet anyway. Not until they had investigated further. She liked the San boy enormously. He'd almost certainly saved their lives. She didn't want to cause him pain when she might have misheard or misunderstood what Reuben James was saying.

She took a gulp of clean desert air and resolved not to be cross anymore. "You're right," she said, "it doesn't prove anything."

Gift's cell phone beeped. He checked the message. "Typical. The camera lens has just been delivered to the hotel. I'll need to go back for it. I'll drop you at the

Welcome Center café and you can have lunch and tour the Stone Age engravings while I'm gone."

He pulled up outside a low, stone building set against a rocky mountain. It was mid-afternoon and the oven blast of desert heat that engulfed Martine as she stepped out of the vehicle threatened to roast her alive.

"Wait," called Martine as Gift prepared to drive away. "Did you have a chance to speak to your guide friend? Did he know anything about Angel's past?"

"Unfortunately not. He's never heard of any zoo in Damaraland, much less one that went out of business. But he did say something that might interest you. Not long after he started in the job three or four years ago, he disturbed Reuben in the midst of a blazing row with Lurk about his mistreatment of an animal, although which animal they were referring to he had no idea. The reason it stuck in his mind is that Lurk cornered him later and told him that it would be 'big mistake' for him to ever repeat what he'd overheard; that his job could be in jeopardy."

Gift glanced at his watch. "I really do have to go. We'll talk later."

"When?" Martine shouted as he reversed. "When will you be back?"

But Gift didn't seem to hear her. "See you soon," he mouthed, and then he was gone and the blanketing heat was closing in on them once again.

Ben sprinkled salt and pepper on his toasted cheese and tomato sandwich, prepared by a smiling cook in the Welcome Center café and purchased with money donated by Gift, took a bite, and started a list on the back of a Damaraland postcard. "We have a million questions, but these are the most important," he said. "Number one: Is Reuben James the rightful inheritor of Sawubona or is he a con artist?"

"A con artist," Martine answered at once.

"We have to be objective, like real detectives," Ben reminded her. "He's not my favorite person either, but Gift thinks highly of him and we should take that into account."

Martine stirred her "Peace" drink, a refreshing blend of *rooibos* tea, orange and lemon juice, and cinnamon, so vigorously that the tourist couple at the next table looked over. As far as she was concerned, if Reuben James was involved in something so explosive it could lead to a war, he was as wicked as she'd thought he was all along. After Gift had gone, she'd filled Ben in on the details of the scene she'd witnessed at Hoodia Haven.

"It sounds as if this man Callum is blackmailing Reuben James," Ben had said. "It's as though he wants to start a fight against Reuben's wishes. But surely they weren't talking about a real war? Maybe it's just an expression and they were using strong language because they were angry."

Martine wasn't convinced. "Hopefully. I'd hate my grandmother to turn on the news in England to find that war has broken out in Namibia and we've both been blown to smithereens."

Then she said, "Maybe the second question on your list should be: If Reuben James and Callum do start a war, who are they going to be attacking?"

Ben scribbled it down. "We also need to find out what the Ark Project is and what it has to do with global warming."

"Question number four: Who broke into the house at Sawubona and what were they looking for?" put in Martine. "Oh, and we still have to find out the truth about the elephant's tale, although I'd be willing to bet that the conversation Gift's friend overheard was about Angel."

"Last one," said Ben. "Are the fairy circles causing the elephants to vanish through: A) Radiation sickness B) Starvation (global warming) C) Aliens! D) The ground is swallowing them (e.g., Bermuda Triangle)?"

He pushed the postcard over to Martine. "All we ever get is more questions. After a week of trying we don't have a single answer."

Martine read the list while sipping at her Peace drink. "It's as if someone's thrown a million jigsaw pieces in the air and we're expected to put them together without knowing what the picture looks like."

"And we've got four days to do it in."

"Four days," Martine said despondently. Sometimes the sheer scale of the mission they'd taken on overwhelmed her.

Ben finished his sandwich and went through the list one more time. "There's a pattern here and we're just not seeing it." He checked his watch. "I'm surprised Gift's not back yet, but there's no point in us sitting around moping. Let's do a tour of the rock engravings. Maybe they'll inspire us."

Martine's spirits rose as soon as they set off up the path that led to the work of the Stone Age artists. The rocks that weren't engraved were, in a way, even more fascinating than those that were. They were riven with swirls, loops, and hollows, as if they'd been sculpted by ocean waves and wild gales.

"That is exactly what has happened," said Edison, their guide. He was a lean, angular man, neatly turned out in a khaki ranger's uniform, who could as easily have been thirty as sixty. Years of guiding had not dulled his passion for his job. He looked at Martine, who was fanning herself with the postcard. "You are hot today, yes?"

"Yes," she responded fervently.

Edison grinned. "Would you believe that hundreds of millions of years ago this entire area was covered in ice? It is incredible, is it not? Later, when the polar ice caps melted and the sea level rose . . ."

"Isn't that what's happening now with global warming?" said Ben. "The polar ice caps are melting and the seas are rising?"

"Exactly," agreed Edison, pleased to be guiding such

a bright boy. "Only at that time it was a good thing. The climate became warmer and many species of flora and fauna thrived in the new lakes, rivers, and swamps. We think that in the Jurassic period, about a hundred eighty to two hundred million years ago, when dinosaurs roamed the Twyfelfontein Valley, this area was a swampy lake."

Martine, who was eleven and three-quarters, found it impossible to get her head around the idea that the Etjo sandstone boulders she was standing among were hundreds of millions of years old, as old as the dinosaurs that had lumbered around them. It made her feel as insignificant as a grain of sand. Whether or not she and Ben managed to save Sawubona, the boulders would still be here—would, in all likelihood, be here for another millennium.

Farther along the path were split boulders, which had provided the Stone Age artists with canvases of perfect sandstone. It was on these that they'd engraved striking images of elephants, rhinoceroses, lions, ostriches, and antelopes, though Martine was pleased to note that their favorite animal seemed to be the giraffe. Edison explained that, to the ancient artists, the giraffe was a symbol of rain. Often they were accompanied by a rainbow and clouds.

The sight of so many giraffes brought on another bout of homesickness. Martine missed Jemmy so much it was like a constant, nagging ache in her heart. Every hour in Namibia had been dogged by the fear that she might never see him again; that by pursuing this quest, she might very well be squandering her last precious days with her beloved white giraffe.

She wondered what Jemmy was doing now and if he was thinking of her. Was he missing her? She hoped that Angel would encourage him to hide in his old sanctuary, far from the prying eyes of the strangers working at Sawubona until she returned, and that Khan was deep inside the warren of tunnels himself. She and her grandmother had pledged to keep the leopard safe from harm on their game reserve. How could they protect him if they no longer lived there?

These thoughts went around and around in Martine's head.

The engravings also made her nostalgic for the Memory Cave at Sawubona. There, however, the paintings were made from Bushman tinctures like oxgall and iron. The Damaraland images had been painstakingly chipped out of the rock and were up to 20,000 years old.

It was while Martine and Ben were examining them that they noticed a series of circles carved into the sandstone. "Edison," Martine called. "Are these fairy circles? Did the Stone Age artists have a theory about how the circles came to be there?"

The guide came over. "Those are not fairy circles. They are engravings of Moon Valley—an extinct volcano crater that the locals believe is haunted." He pointed. "Look, you can see it from here."

Across the valley, interrupting the crooked line of

purple mountains, was a charred hill shaped like a funnel.

"A local businessman, Reuben James, is building a nature oasis there, and there are many who believe he is most unwise. They think the spirits will be displeased."

Martine was startled. "Did you say *Reuben James* is building a nature oasis there?"

Edison looked at her sharply. "You know him?"

"We don't like him," Martine responded, unwilling to go into how or why she and Ben were acquainted with Mr. James.

He nodded sympathetically. "I myself am not sure how I feel about this man. He has done many good things for people and animals in this area, but this new project, there is something wrong with it. It is causing much unhappiness with the locals."

"I thought Mr. James was very popular around here," said Ben.

"He was, and for many people he still is. But the building of this hotel has created much controversy. In order to create his oasis, he will require many gallons of water from the fresh-water spring the Damara people call *Ui-Ais*. It means 'a water place where the stones stand clustered together.' For thousands of years, the people and animals of this area have depended on this spring for survival. Now it is under threat.

"And that is not the only thing. Unemployment is high in Damaraland and yet there are no local workers there. They are from faraway places like Windhoek or Etosha, or foreigners from Zambia or Botswana."

"I can see why that would cause resentment," said Ben. "When is the oasis due to open?"

"Soon, but if you want me to be honest, I don't think it will happen. There are rumors that Mr. James has big, big debts that are getting worse by the day, but in my opinion this is not the only reason."

Martine squinted across the valley. A dust-caked truck was beetling across the dusty plain toward Moon Valley. It disappeared into the haze. "Then why?"

Edison picked up a smooth stone and turned it over and over in his palm. He lowered his voice. "Maybe it's a strong word, but I'm sure there is something evil about this project. There are stories that if you complain about the building work or how near it is to the stream or ask too many questions about Moon Valley, bad things will happen to you. We had this man living in Damaraland, an elephant whisperer. A year ago he went missing and not even one footprint of his has been found."

Martine saw Ben's eyes widen at the mention of Gift's father.

"The last place he was seen was at the gates of Moon Valley."

22

By sunset, Gift still had not returned. The Welcome Center closed, and Martine and Ben found a perch on a hillock a short distance away, from where they could see the road and parking lot but would not attract the attention of any well-meaning departing staff who might insist on calling their parents.

"It's very unfair of him to leave us here for hours on end," moaned Martine, wriggling into her sweatshirt. As if a switch had been turned off, the chill of the desert night was moving in. "What on earth can he be up to? Do you think he's eating a three-course dinner at the hotel? When he shows up, I'm really going to tell him off."

"*If* he shows up," said Ben.

Martine stared at him. It was a possibility that hadn't occurred to her. "But he *has* to come back. He promised to help. Surely he wouldn't abandon us here?"

"Who knows? It's not as if he owes us anything. We're going after a man he obviously likes and respects. Why should he help us? We're also trouble, in the sense that we've entered Namibia illegally and my parents and your grandmother don't know where we are. Maybe he's decided to get out while the going is good. It's not like we could find him again."

"But we know where he lives."

"Do we? Could you locate that place again? We should have asked for his phone number, but it didn't occur to me we'd need it."

Another thought came into Martine's head. "Ben, what if something's happened to him? What if he went back to the hotel and that ghastly Lurk was lurking and pounced on him? He'll be dying to get revenge for the gift shop incident. He's sly, that man. I wouldn't trust him as far as I could throw him. Why does Reuben James employ him?"

"That's what I mean," said Ben. "All we ever get is more questions. It's about time we found an answer."

It's hard to say which of them first came up with the plan to search Moon Valley, but in the end it didn't matter. As far as they were concerned, they'd gambled with their own fate and that of Sawubona by coming to Namibia, by throwing in their lot with Gift, by pursuing Reuben James. If they didn't finish what they'd started, it would all have been for nothing.

For hour upon hour they'd watched for the headlights of Gift's vehicle to illuminate the Welcome Center parking lot, but nothing split the star-showered darkness. They wrapped themselves in the space blanket for warmth and took turns dozing, getting up when Ben's watch alarm went off at three a.m., stiff, sore, cold, and worried. They'd nibbled a bit of hoodia cactus to stave off hunger pangs and thirst, but they couldn't help but feel agitated about their friend.

There were two likely explanations for Gift's continuing absence, neither of them good. Either he'd betrayed them by deliberately dumping them at the Welcome Center in the belief that staff there would rescue them or call the police. Or something terrible had befallen him. Martine pictured him bleeding by the roadside after overturning his four-wheel drive on the slippery gravel road.

"I'd feel a lot better if there was some way we could leave a message for Gift," said Ben. "You know, in case he comes looking for us."

Martine looked at the flat, dark valley and ring of black mountains. The moon was on the rise, and the stars winked and shimmered. "I have an idea. We *can* leave him a message!" she told him, remembering something Gift had said about the way desert people communicated in the absence of phones and computers. "Help me gather up the lightest stones you can find."

Minutes later they'd left their first desert telegraph—a white giraffe made of stones, its long neck pointing in the direction they planned to travel. They planned to leave one every couple of hundred yards.

They headed out across the plain, their flashlight lighting a yellow path across the scrub, shale, and rocks.

As they walked, Ben said, "We don't have to do this, you know. We could turn around now and go back to the

Welcome Center. Yes, we'll be in loads of trouble and the police will be called and Gwyn Thomas will hit the roof and my mum and dad will refuse to allow me out of their sight ever again, but it'll be worth it because we'll be safe. We'll be *alive*."

Martine glanced sideways at him. "Do *you* want to turn back?"

"Only if you do."

"Well, I don't. If there's a chance—even a microscopic one—that by going to Moon Valley and finding out what Reuben James is up to we could save Sawubona and Jemmy and Khan, then that's what I have to do . . . Hey, did you see that?"

The crater had lit up, as if the volcano had come to life. At the same time they heard a muffled rumble, like distant thunder. Then it went dark and quiet again.

"Great," said Martine. "Like we haven't been through enough. Now we have the prospect of being incinerated by a smoldering volcano to look forward to."

Ben grinned. "Hardly. This is an extinct volcano. What we heard was a man-made explosion that was probably caused by the dynamite we saw on the plane. Wouldn't you rather be blown sky high than boiled alive in bubbling orange lava?"

"Those are my options?" said Martine. "Gee, let me think. Oh, there is another one. I could beat you up."

She made a fist and chased after him and the two of them ran through the desert laughing, and briefly forgot about their troubles.

They'd reached a cluster of fairy circles when Ben said, "I'm sure this is the spot where the elephant disappeared in Gift's photograph. I recognize that line of boulders, because they look like a face with a missing tooth."

Martine was doubtful. "Ben, there are millions of fairly circles. Even supposing you're right, what does it mean?"

"Well, nothing unless you think about how coincidental it is that Gift's father and at least one elephant disappeared very close to Moon Valley."

"Ben, that's crazy. I can't stand Reuben James, but you're accusing him of kidnapping Gift's dad. Surely even he wouldn't do something so wicked. Would he?"

She turned to look at the volcanic crater. The burnt slopes loomed before them like the dark side of the moon. There was a phosphorescent glow emanating from it, as if it was lit from within in the manner of a football stadium. "What he doesn't know isn't going to hurt him," Reuben James had said about Gift. Later, his crow-haired companion had virtually blackmailed him into doing whatever it took to ensure the Ark Project was a success. Men like that would surely stop at nothing.

Martine switched off her flashlight. "I guess we'd better proceed with extreme caution."

23

The sky was lightening as they scaled the gritty rim of the crater and wriggled on their bellies toward the edge. By that time they were so filthy they looked as if they'd spent a week in a coal mine. They had considered attempting to get in through the main gate, which they'd seen from a distance as they approached, but it was three times their height, made of iron and set into the crater wall. It was also patrolled by two security guards with dogs.

As they inched forward, their eyes, which had grown accustomed to the dark, burned with the brightness of the glare below. Martine shielded hers and peered over the brink of the volcano. At first all she could see was fizzing white spotlights bent, like preying mantis, over a valley. When her eyes finally adjusted, she gasped. Of all the things she'd expected to find, this was not it. She had expected construction site chaos and men toiling away with cranes, concrete mixers, and scaffolding. In her wilder thoughts, she'd even envisioned a training facility for soldiers preparing for Callum's "war." And when Edison spoke of Reuben James's plan to create an oasis, she'd pictured three tired palm trees leaning over a concrete pool enlivened with a few fake pink flamingos.

She hadn't imagined a tropical jungle festooned with flowering vines and crisscrossed with wooden walkways. Or a crystal blue fountain. Or clouds of brilliant color floating over beds of African wildflowers, which, when Ben got out his little binoculars, they saw were butterflies as bright as jewels. She definitely hadn't foreseen a futuristic hotel made from wood and glass and suspended in the treetops, or a maze of the type one might find at a castle in England, with an okapi—a beautiful little creature with zebra-striped hind legs, which is a close cousin of the giraffe—tripping through it.

She'd never imagined they'd stumble on paradise in the most unlikely place in Africa.

"What do you reckon goes on in there?" asked Ben.

Martine followed his gaze. At the far end of the valley, barely visible through the trees, was a dome of opaque white. It resembled a giant golf ball.

"It looks a lot like the Eden Project, this place my mum and dad used to take me to in England. Sounds similar to the Ark Project, doesn't it? The domes there are massive greenhouses that house rainforests and waterfalls and all kinds of things. That might be what they're doing here."

A splash of red appeared in the fading night sky. As if on cue, a sublime chorus of birdsong floated up to them. A gardener in overalls appeared and began tending to the wildflowers.

"Wow," said Martine. "Wow, wow, wow!"

"I'm confused," she said to Ben as they scrambled back down the slope. "Every time I think Reuben James is Mr. Hyde, he turns into Dr. Jekyll."

Ben put out a hand to steady her as she slipped on a loose rock. "Meaning what exactly?"

"Well, every time I decide that he's a kidnapper, or a con man, or a burglar, or an elephant poacher, he does something unexpected. Like the time he lent us his new Land Rover so we could help the sick buffalo. And now this. Ben, isn't Moon Valley one of the most idyllic places you've ever seen? But I didn't see any elephants. I'm losing hope that, with days to go, we'll find anything on Reuben James so bad it'll stop him taking over Sawubona."

"What he's done with Moon Valley is incredible," said Ben, "but there are too many things that don't add up. If he has this place as well as Hoodia Haven and others, why is he so obsessed with taking over Sawubona? Sawubona is special to us, but there are a thousand game reserves just like it. Yet he's fixated on ours. Don't worry, we'll get something on Reuben James yet. But we're going to need to find a way into Moon Valley."

"Why don't we take a closer look at the delivery area?" suggested Martine. Earlier, they'd seen a red-lettered sign directing drivers to the drop zone. They were to contact the site office on arrival, using the telephone provided.

"Yes, let's look at the drop zone," said Ben. "There might be cargo waiting to be transferred to Moon Valley and we could hide in a box and get in that way. That always works in movies."

They ran along the curve of the crater until they were at the opposite end of the valley to the main gate, level, Martine estimated, with the white dome. The "drop zone" was a circular area of cleared gravel, ground up by thick tire tracks, and a ramshackle warehouse.

"If it's a storage unit, why isn't it guarded?" whispered Martine.

"It could be that guards aren't necessary," Ben told her. "If the trucks are unloaded and their cargo moved to Moon Valley minutes later, the goods are under observation the whole time."

To be on the safe side, they waited a while longer before approaching the warehouse, but saw no one. As Ben had predicted, it was empty. The concrete floor had been swept clean. There was a framed poster of a charging elephant on one wall and a desk and chair near the doorway. A grubby black telephone, clipboard, and pen had been provided. A notice requested that visitors "Dial 9 for Site Office."

"We could ring and say we have a delivery," said Martine.

Ben was staring at the elephant poster. "Too risky for too little reward. I'm not confident I could make myself sound like a fifty-year-old Namibian truck driver on the phone. Martine, don't you think it's a bit odd that they've decided to decorate this dusty old warehouse?"

Martine sat down on the chair and began flicking through the pages on the clipboard. The previous day there had been deliveries of bread, milk, fertilizer, and twenty vials of medicine. Marine recognized the name of it, but couldn't for the life of her remember what it was for. "Perhaps they were trying to be welcoming."

"Or conceal something." Ben pushed the poster aside. Behind it was a green lever. "Hey Martine, look at this. It has fresh oil on it, as if it's regularly in use. I wonder what it does."

He tugged at it.

"No!" cried Martine, but it was too late. Before Ben could react, a trapdoor had dropped open beneath his feet. Ben dropped with it. Martine had a fleeting glimpse of his startled face as he twisted away down a chute, then the mechanism purred and the trapdoor snapped shut again.

Twice before in her life Martine had felt a terror so extreme that it was as if she'd been turned into a block of ice. Once was on the night of the fire, and the second time was when she fell into a shark-infested ocean. Now she felt it again.

This could not be happening. She could not have just watched her best friend vanish. She could not be left alone with no food, water, money, passport, or transport in the middle of the Namib desert.

This could not be happening—but, her fevered brain told her, it was.

She was faced with two choices. Either she walked back to the Welcome Center, waited for it to open, and attempted to call the police, who might arrest her for entering the country illegally and refuse to listen to her pleas for assistance.

Or she could pull the lever and follow Ben into a void from which they might never emerge.

She knew which was the smarter choice. She also knew that it would take her a minimum of forty-five minutes to run back to the Welcome Center when she was already weak from hunger and thirst. By then, her best friend, whom she now realized she loved as much as she did Jemmy, her grandmother, Grace, Tendai, and Khan, might have been consumed by whatever it was that waited at the bottom of the chute.

What *did* wait there? Martine had visions of an underground stream packed with piranhas or a bottomless shaft that went to the molten center of the earth. But even those would be preferable to ending up in the hands of Reuben James and Callum.

So there was the wise decision, or the decision she could make because Ben was her best friend and there was nothing she wouldn't do for him. For Martine, there was no contest. She gathered up some pale stones and made another white giraffe, which she laid on the ground behind the warehouse. By some miracle, Gift might stumble across it.

The sky was streaked with pinks and grays and oranges as Martine returned to the stifling shed and pulled the lever. The mechanism gave a small sigh, as if resigning itself to dispatching yet another victim. Her stomach lurched in fear.

The trapdoor snapped open and she was swallowed.

24

Martine had never understood the appeal of roller coasters. It was beyond her why anyone would want their stomach left behind while their body plummeted like a human cannonball and their heart threatened to burst from their chest. Unfortunately, that's the exact sensation she was experiencing now.

Teeth gritted, she hurtled down a silver chute, flailing helplessly around the corners. Time passed in dentist minutes, the way it did when she was having a filling and the dentist was leaning on her jaw with his drill and talking about his beach holiday with his family while the nurse sprayed water up her nose. She'd have preferred time to go in giraffe minutes. When she was out in the game reserve with Jemmy, whole nights went in the blink of an eye.

Martine popped from the tube like a cork from a bottle and hit the ground hard. It was a relief to find it was cushioned. A soft landing area had been installed to prevent fragile deliveries from being damaged. And if there was one thing Martine was feeling, it was fragile.

She dusted herself off and stood up. She was in a neon-lit room, empty apart from a hotel housekeeping trolley, a sink, and a row of white coats on pegs. There was a door but no windows. An iron-rung ladder rose to meet a hatch in the ceiling overhead. She was trying to decide which exit Ben might have taken when she heard footsteps approaching the door. At the same time, a hand clamped over her mouth.

"Martine, whatever you do, don't scream," Ben whispered in her ear. "I'll wedge something under the door to keep it closed. Go up the ladder."

Martine recovered from her fright and rushed to do as he said. A key scraped in the lock. Ben had wedged a broom handle under it, but it was already splintering as he shinned up the ladder and clambered out into the morning sunshine.

Two gardeners were trimming the maze not fifty feet away from them. Fortunately, they were talking and didn't hear anything above the buzz of the hedge trimmers. Martine and Ben had a split second to take in the vivid beauty of the oasis—the brilliant beds of flowers; the cool blue fountain and the soaring, creeper-hung forest rising up a slope toward the white dome; the hotel nestled among its branches like a human version of a community weaverbird nest—and then they were diving into the maze.

Once again, they seemed to have got away with it. They ran along the dewy green passages, backtracking whenever they came to a dead end. They wanted to get as far away from the gardeners as they could before pausing to come up with a plan. The hedges, thick as castle walls, muffled nearly all noise apart from the birdsong, which was as continuous and cheerful as ever.

"You know what's really peculiar," whispered Ben, "I haven't seen a single bird since we got here. Yet they're chirping and whistling so loudly it's as if we've walked into an aviary."

"Maybe they're hidden in the jungle," said Martine, but goose bumps rose on her arms. There was something creepy about Moon Valley. It was too impossibly perfect.

She wondered where the okapi was. Thinking about him reminded her of Jemmy, and her chest began to ache again. How many days, or weeks, would it be till she saw him again? *Would* she ever see him again?

Ben squeezed through a narrow gap between the hedges and stopped so abruptly Martine ran into him. In the square center of the maze was a table spread with a starched white cloth and laid with shining silverware and white china plates. On it was a breakfast feast of fruit, apricot juice, water, a selection of cheeses and jams, and a basket of bakery goods. The basket was upended and its contents, fat, buttery croissants, chocolate chip and banana nut muffins, and health breads, were strewn across the tablecloth.

The okapi, which had its front hooves on the table, was gleefully nibbling a muffin and didn't notice them at first. When it did, it bounded away guiltily, leaving a trail of crumbs in its path.

There was only one chair and a single place laid.

"Are you thinking what I'm thinking?" said Ben.

Martine grinned. "Well, my first thought was, this has to be Reuben James's breakfast. My second is, now it's ours!"

"Martine, you're a mind reader." Ben reached for a roll and spread it thickly with butter and strawberry jam. He poured himself some apricot juice and drank it looking over his shoulder, aware that Reuben James could already be on his way.

Martine drank two glasses of water and devoured a chocolate chip muffin and a croissant dripping with butter and honey. She said, "You do know that our lives will not be worth living if we get caught?"

"Mmmhmm," Ben mumbled through a mouthful of roll. His eyes were laughing.

Over the relentless singing of the birds came the unmistakable tinkle of cups, saucers, and teaspoons on a tray. Martine and Ben bolted through the gap in the maze just as a waiter stepped into the square and let out a curse. He set down his tray with a crash. "You wicked okapi!" he cried. "Wait until I get my hands on you. Tonight you will be okapi curry. I will serve you up with rice and mango chutney!"

"Okapi curry?" mouthed Martine, horrified.

"If we don't get out of here, we'll be in the same pot," Ben mouthed back. "Follow me."

Earlier he'd spotted a red thread running along the bottom of some sections of the hedge, which appeared to show the way out. They were stealing along a cool green passage, feeling like mice about to be devoured by cats, when Ben tripped over a wire. Instantly the birdsong ceased. An unnatural silence descended on the valley.

"Oh. My. God," whispered Martine. "It's a recording. There *are* no birds in Moon Valley. I guess it *is* haunted after all."

The sudden shutting off of the birdsong CD told the waiter that all was not well in the volcano and that something bigger than the okapi might be to blame for the ruined breakfast. He yelled for the gardeners. They came pounding into the maze, shouting and wielding sticks.

Martine and Ben clung to each other in panic. There was no escape route. Men were coming at them from both directions. They were trapped. The game was up.

From across the desert came the wail of an ambulance siren. It was approaching at speed. All sounds of pursuit ceased. The siren grew louder and louder until it was right inside Moon Valley, where it petered out with a squawk.

Ben peered through a hole in the hedge. "Martine, you have to see this."

Martine crouched beside him. The ambulance men were carrying a stretcher up the forest paths to the white dome. A door opened and two men in white coats lifted out a bloodied figure, plainly unconscious. The paramedics laid him on the stretcher, checked his pulse, and then whisked him back down the hill.

The gardeners, the waiter, and the men in white coats gathered around the ambulance, watching with anxious faces as the paramedics attempted to stabilize the injured man.

"Ben, this is our chance," said Martine.

Crouching low, they sprinted from the maze to the hatch. In the storage room below, Ben put on a white coat and used the sink to wash the volcanic dust off his face and hands. Martine was about to do the same, but he stopped her.

"I might be able to pass as a worker, but I don't think a girl will. *But,*" he added hastily as Martine opened her mouth to protest, "I have a solution."

He slid back the curtain on the trolley, removed a pile of towels, and shoved them out of sight beneath the sink. It was a tight squeeze, but Martine managed to wedge herself in.

The hatch opened and a man in a white coat slid down the ladder like a fireman down a pole. He was bald and wearing milk-bottle glasses. His hands were large and hairy. Ben closed the trolley curtain calmly.

"Who are you?" the man demanded. "Why are you wearing a white coat? Those are only for pod workers."

"I'm the new cleaner, sir," said Ben. "I apologize if I'm in the wrong clothes. I was still waiting for my instructions when I received an urgent call to mop up . . . to remove some *blood.*" He whispered the last word.

The man grimaced. "Good thing it's less than twenty-four hours till they're gone. Any longer and we'd have a dead body on our hands. If you want my opinion, the old man is losing control. He's the real deal, but he's not a magician."

Ben filled the bucket with soap and water and whipped it into foam with a mop. "Losing control?"

"Of the elephants," the man said impatiently. "What else? They've been cooped up so long they're on the verge of rampaging."

25

"The *elephants?*" Martine said, pulling aside her trolley curtain and trying to wriggle into a more comfortable position. Her left foot had gone to sleep. After the pod worker had helpfully typed in the keypad security code and held the door open for Ben, he'd rushed on ahead, leaving them to negotiate a long tunnel with solar lighting. "That means there's more than two and there could be a whole herd. I guess we've found your Bermuda Triangle, only it's a white dome in an extinct volcano with fake birdsong."

"Shh," said Ben, closing her curtain firmly. "I'm not sure this is a good idea. It would make more sense for us to try to get out of Moon Valley and get help. We don't want to end up like the man on the stretcher."

"Of course it's not a good idea," retorted Martine. "It's a terrible idea. But we've come this far. We can't turn back now. The elephants need us."

The explosion they'd heard in the desert sounded again; only down here it was an express train roar, booming down the corridor. It didn't last long, and when it was over

160

they heard a discordant hammering. Then that too ceased.

For all her brave words, Martine was cold with fear. She and Ben had traveled thousands of miles and risked everything to try to uncover the truth about Angel's story and investigate Reuben James's business dealings. Faced with learning the answers, she realized they might be more than she could bear.

She focused on Jemmy. "I will get back to him, I will get back to him, I will get back to him," she told herself over and over, like a mantra.

The trolley halted. She heard Ben take a deep breath. "We're here," he said. "Ready?"

Martine wriggled her toes in an effort to restore sensation to her foot. "Ready."

Once, many years ago, Martine's mum and dad had taken her to a gallery in London. The spirit-lifting paintings of Turner, Van Gogh, and other old masters had made such an impression on her that she'd briefly entertained the idea of becoming an artist, but one picture had depressed her—a vision of hell by Hieronymus Bosch. The artist's name had stuck in her head because she couldn't understand what sort of parents would name their child Hieronymus.

Peering through a slit in the compartment curtain, she was reminded of it. It's not that it actually looked like hell. Far from it. Two-thirds of the vast dome had been transformed into the most remarkable indoor environment any desert elephant could have wished for. Whole dunes had been transported intact, and in between there were acacia trees, a small baobab hung with cream of tartar pods (an elephant treat), and a muddy pond for them to swim in. There was even an elephant play area, with colored balls, sticks, and bells. The roof of the dome had been painted sky blue and had wisps of cloud on it and a few painted birds.

It wasn't the fake desert that caused Martine such anguish; it was the elephants. There were nineteen of them. All were shackled and all were exhibiting signs of distress. Some were swaying listlessly, eyes half-closed, as if they were lost in a world of their own. One was aggressively destroying an acacia tree, another was feeling every inch of the walls of the dome with her trunk in the vain hope of finding a way out. The rest were just shuffling back and forth in their shackles, variously bored, depressed, or agitated.

As Martine gazed out on the diabolical scene, a pair of white doors opened in the far wall. She caught a glimpse of a laboratory behind, with rows of test tubes and blinking machines. There was a horrible rattling and a steel cage was wheeled out by two white-coated workers. Inside was an elephant. One of the workers pulled a lever and the elephant burst out, was caught short by her shackles, and fell to her knees.

A gaunt man with fine features and caramel-colored skin rushed from the shadows and ran to her side. He was the only person not in a white coat, and his loose trousers and shirt were thin and worn. He stroked the elephant's wrinkled gray-brown face and tried to soothe her. When a lab worker tried to approach, he sent him away. Gently, he urged the elephant to her feet.

"Gift's father," Martine breathed.

26

"We've got to get out of here and get help," whispered Ben. "I'm not sure what's going on here, but we're in way over our heads."

"Animal experimentation, that's what's going on," Martine said furiously. It took all her self-restraint not to leap out of the trolley. "If we don't find a way to stop it, that's what Reuben James will be doing to Jemmy—experimenting on him. And Gift's father, the so-called elephant whisperer, is involved."

"You don't know that."

"What else would he be doing in this hideous place? It's not *him* that's being kept prisoner and tortured in the lab, is it?"

"Just because he isn't in handcuffs, doesn't mean he's not a prisoner," Ben pointed out.

"Oi, you? What are you looking at?" A short, stocky pod worker was striding across the dome. "Where's your ID? What are you doing here?"

"Leave him alone, Nipper," called the bald man. "It's his first day on the job. Hey, kid, what's your name?"

"Ben."

"All righty, Ben, get your mop and head on over to the lab."

"Yes, sir!" called Ben. Under his breath he said: "This is about to get very complicated." He pushed the trolley forward.

Martine risked another glance through the curtain. Gift's father was leading the traumatized elephant to the muddy pool. Her stride was uncertain and her eyes were locked on Gift's dad, as if he were a lighthouse in a storm.

Martine realized with a shock that the second part of Grace's prophecy had just come to pass. The circle—the Moon Valley volcano, that is—*had* led to the elephants. Now all that remained was the last part. "The elephants will lead you to the truth," Grace had promised. *"Your* truth." Now that she might be on the brink of discovering that truth, Martine wasn't sure she wanted to know the answer. What if she didn't like it? What if the truth was more painful than the not knowing?

One of the elephants trumpeted. The sound ricocheted around the dome and blasted Martine's eardrums. The ailing elephant had collapsed again, only this time she wasn't getting up. Gift's father was cradling her head. All around the dome, elephants were straining at their shackles and flapping their ears or tossing their tusks, desperate to go to the aid of their fallen friend.

"Ben, we have to do something," said Martine, forgetting to keep her voice down. Patience was not one of her virtues.

"Martine, if we run back down the tunnel, we might still be able to get out of here, expose this whole operation, and save all the elephants. If we stay here, we might not save any. We might not even—"

Martine hopped out of the trolley, staggering a little on her cramped, bloodless limbs. "Save ourselves? Is that what you were going to say? Well, right now all I care about is saving her. What's going on here is like something out of the Dark Ages. We can't just walk away."

Ben glanced in the direction of the fallen elephant. The bald man and two other pod workers were preoccupied with the unfolding crisis. Another man had retreated to the safety of the laboratory. However, Nipper was staring at the intruders with intense interest. He took a cell phone from his pocket.

"Ben, go without me," urged Martine. "Find Gift or call the police and come back for me."

"Not a chance. We came into this together and we're going to stay together. But I think one of the workers has just called security. We'll have to move fast."

Martine had the advantage of surprise. By the time Nipper had alerted the other pod workers that a thin, pale girl with flying brown hair and green eyes was racing across the dome, she was almost upon them.

She slowed to a walk. She didn't underestimate what she was about to do. Her gift was her most precious secret. She'd first discovered she could heal animals purely by accident, on a class trip. Afterward, the children who'd witnessed her revival of an Egyptian goose had chased her through a forest, screaming, "Witch! Witch! Witch!"

Since then she'd been very careful to hide her gift from everyone but Grace and Ben, and even with them she played it down. Now she was about to attempt a healing in front of an audience. Nipper tried to grab her but the bald man stopped him.

"Wait. Let's see what she's going to do."

Nipper folded his muscled arms across his chest and a smug smile came over his swarthy face. Ben, who was hovering anxiously nearby, noticed that his gaze kept shifting to the door.

Gift's father was still cradling the elephant's head. He lifted weary, hurt-filled eyes when Martine knelt down.

"Do you mind if I try to help her, Joseph?" Martine asked. He started when she said his name, but nodded dumbly. The elephant's thick lashes lay flat against her rough gray-brown cheek. Her whole body trembled. When Martine touched her tenderly, a tear rolled down her face.

Unzipping her survival kit, Martine took out the bottle labeled "Love Potion No. 9." Grace had explained to her that it was the plant equivalent of Adrenalin, only to be given in extreme emergencies when the heart was failing. But some sixth sense told Martine that the elephant's heart was failing not because she was having a cardiac arrest, but because it had been broken. Her freedom and family had been stolen from her. She had nothing left to live for.

Martine returned the bottle to the pouch without opening it. She would have to trust in her gift alone. She laid her hands on the elephant's heart. "What do you call her?" she asked Joseph.

"Ruby," the elephant whisperer told her. "I call her Ruby."

Martine barely heard him. Already the gawking faces were swirling away from her and her hands were so hot her blood was virtually boiling in her veins. Most times when she healed an animal Martine had dreamlike visions of warriors with spears and great herds of animals and men in animal masks. Today she saw Sawubona.

She was standing by the water hole in front of her grandmother's house. Jemmy was at her right shoulder and Angel at her left, and the savannah was surface-lit with a golden light, the way it was when a storm threatened. Martine had a strong feeling the animals were trying to tell her something. She put a hand on Angel's trunk and the elephant's unspoken words came to her as clearly as if they'd been written on her soul with indelible ink: "Bring me my sister. Bring me my sister."

"Where is your sister? Where do I find her?" asked Martine, but Angel's words were lost in the wind.

Martine pressed her face to Jemmy's silver muzzle. She could feel its silky softness against her cheek. "I love you. Come home soon," he told her in his wordless, musical way.

She was in the midst of saying "I love you too," when applause cut short her trance. She came around in a daze to find that Ruby was on her feet. She was swaying, but the light had returned to her mournful brown eyes. With the tip of her trunk she caressed Martine's cheek in an elephant kiss. Moved beyond words, Martine kissed her back.

She stood up, suddenly self-conscious. She was afraid to look behind her; afraid to think what might happen next.

Joseph was speaking, his voice was barely audible. "Not much surprises me these days, miss, but you have truly amazed me. I wonder if I am dreaming, but I fear I will wake soon enough in this nightmare without end. How did you know my name?"

"Hey, how did you do that?" interrupted the bald man. "We need some of that medicine you gave her. That's some kind of a miracle cure. Who are you, anyway? Reuben's niece?"

A heavy hand slammed down on Martine's shoulder and Nipper wrenched her around, almost knocking the bald man over.

Before her, looking rather more tired than the last time she'd seen him but wearing the same sardonic, confident smile, was Reuben James.

"So Martine," he said, "we meet again."

27

Without waiting for her to reply, he went on: "I must say these are not quite the circumstances in which I imagined our paths next crossing, but it's always a pleasure to meet a worthy adversary."

Martine wriggled out of Nipper's grasp and glared at her archenemy. "The feeling's not mutual."

He laughed at that. Incensed, Martine said, "I suppose you think it's funny that an elephant almost died just then because she's so traumatized by your experiments. It's one thing stealing Sawubona out from under us, but I didn't think even you could stoop so low as to masquerade as a caring conservationist when you're nothing but an animal torturer."

That brought another smile to his lips. "Torture? Is that what you think we're doing here? Martine, you have me all wrong. We're doing the complete opposite. These elephants undergo the occasional blood test and go the odd day without food or water so we can study their endurance levels, but their sacrifice is nothing compared to the rewards that will be reaped by future generations of elephants. And though they may not understand it, many of these particular elephants owe their lives to me. Out in the desert, they might already have been killed by poachers, or have died of hunger and thirst."

He paused as one of the pod workers came up with Ben, his arm twisted behind his back. Reuben James frowned at the man. "Matheus, what are you thinking? Release him at once. He's only a boy."

Ben rushed to Martine's side, rubbing his arm to get the blood flowing. Martine put a protective hand on his shoulder and glared at Reuben James. "Ruby doesn't owe her life to you," she snapped. "She almost lost it because of you. And I suppose Angel was caged and experimented on until she was broken and bleeding too. That's why you sent her to Sawubona. That's why you lied about her coming from a zoo that had shut down."

Reuben James looked mystified until she said the last part. "You're talking about the elephant I sent to Sawubona? Angel? Is that what you call her? Yes, well, that was very unfortunate. It happened in the early stages of our development, when we were still learning the ropes, as it were. She was our test case and we didn't yet have this custom-built facility. I'd hired Lurk—you remember my chauffeur?—to supervise the early experiments. Let's just say he was overzealous and that particular elephant, Angel, was impossible to handle. But regardless of what you might think of me, I can't abide cruelty to animals. Lurk was severely reprimanded and transferred to another position. We ceased all experiments until about a year ago, when the dome was completed and the Moon Valley oasis was well on its way."

He jerked his chin in Joseph's direction. "That's when we brought in the elephant whisperer."

"Brought him in?" scoffed Martine. "Kidnapped him, you mean?"

"Martine, why do you persist in seeing me as a villain? Do you see handcuffs? He can leave at any time. He chooses to be here with his beloved elephants, don't you, Joseph?"

Joseph nodded quickly and busied himself giving a bucket of food to Ruby.

"What about your son?" Martine burst out before she could stop herself. "Don't you care about him?" The elephant whisperer flinched as if she'd hit him, but he didn't look around.

Reuben James's eyes narrowed. "How do you know about his son?"

Martine said quickly, "One of the guides at the Stone Age etchings told us that the elephant whisperer had gone missing. He mentioned a son."

Reuben James wasn't convinced, though he didn't argue. "There is a boy, but he's in his late teens now. I've been like a second father to him. That's the agreement we have, Joseph and I. Joseph takes care of the elephants and I take care of his son. I doubt Gift has a bad word to say about me."

He fixed Martine with a brooding look. "Lurk said he saw you in the hotel shop. I didn't believe him."

"Why Sawubona?" asked Ben. "Why not have Angel sent to a sanctuary in Namibia? Why go to the trouble and expense of sending her to another country?"

Reuben James returned his gaze coolly. "To leave her here would have been to risk derailing the Ark Project . . ." He swept an arm across the dome.

"This, by the way, is the Ark Project. We didn't want it shut down when it had hardly begun. As you've rightly pointed out, I have a reputation as a conservationist. If a heavily pregnant elephant with the extensive injuries of Angel had turned up at a sanctuary in Namibia, people would have started asking questions. I'd met your grandfather at a wildlife conference and was impressed by his dedication to animals. I thought that if anyone could save her, it was Henry. Logistically it was a bit of a challenge to get her to South Africa, but we managed in the end."

"Hasn't that worked out well for you?" Martine said sarcastically. "Now you have Angel *and* our game reserve. What a coincidence."

"Not a coincidence, just smart business, Martine. I did your grandfather a good turn and, by passing away without repaying the debt, he unintentionally returned the favor. As it turns out, Sawubona is the perfect location for the South African branch of the Ark Project."

"But why?" cried Martine. "Why *our* home? There a million game reserves where you could perform your awful experiments. Are there diamonds in ours or something?"

Reuben James sighed. "Martine, you disappoint me. I

thought you'd have it figured out by now. The Ark Project has nothing to do with diamonds or gold, or platinum for that matter. It's about something much bigger than that."

"Global warming," Ben put in quietly. "It's about global warming."

"Not bad," drawled Reuben James. "Not bad at all."

"You've lost me," said Martine.

"All right, forget about Sawubona for a moment . . ." Ben said.

As if, thought Martine.

"Remember the Bushman legend the rock seller told us about? The one where God granted their dream of great wealth by turning all of Namibia's lakes and rivers into diamonds?"

"But that's just a fable."

"Yes, but think about it. In a desert country, what could be more valuable than diamonds, gold, and platinum put together?"

"Water?" cried Martine. "That's what this is all about—water?"

She stared around her and a lightbulb finally went off in her head. "That's what you're doing at Moon Valley, isn't it? You're planning to divert the spring that's provided the people and animals of Damaraland with one of their only sources of water for thousands of years, so that you alone can control it. And you've built it in an extinct volcano that local people believe is haunted and stay well away from, in order to do it undetected.

"I suppose the oasis provides extra insurance. It's so beautiful that it would never occur to anyone that, behind the scenes, a devious plot is unfolding."

Reuben James's eyes gleamed with excitement. He seemed to have forgotten their bizarre circumstances or the fact that Martine and Ben were, in effect, trespassers, and was talking to them as if they were interested in buying a stake in his company.

"In the future, as pollution spreads, global warming kicks in, and the heating of the earth's surface leads to an increase in droughts and other extreme weather, more wars will be fought over water than have been fought over oil or religion throughout history. The people who control the water supplies will control the earth."

"So at the end of the day it's about money and power and not about conserving animals or water at all," Martine said.

Reuben James's mouth twitched. "It is possible to do both."

"Is water the reason you want Sawubona so much?" asked Ben. "Because there's a lake in the game reserve?"

Reuben James regarded him with suspicion, as if it had occurred to him for the first time that he might be telling them too much. "Among other things," he answered vaguely.

He glanced at his watch and gestured to the stocky man. "Nipper, do me a favor and take Martine and Ben to the hotel. They're probably not hungry, given that they've already partaken of my breakfast in the maze, but if they are, see that they're given lunch and one of our best rooms for the night."

"Thanks," said Martine, "but we need to be getting back. My grandmother will be worried."

Reuben James chuckled. "I doubt very much that your grandmother knows where you are. Indeed I'm rather keen to know how you got here myself, but we'll save that story for another day."

"You're keeping us prisoner?"

"Don't be absurd. You're free to leave Moon Valley anytime. Anytime, that is, after Christmas Eve, three days from now. You see, that's when Sawubona becomes mine, and I'd hate anything to happen that might interfere with the launch of my new safari park."

28

"If we're free to go, why don't we just walk out of Moon Valley and call the wildlife authorities or Grace and Tendai?" asked Martine. "We might even run into Gift. He might have found our white giraffe stone messages and be out in the desert searching for us."

There was a pause while Ben swallowed a mouthful of steak and fries. To annoy Reuben James, they'd ordered the most expensive items on the room service menu shortly after being shown to a suite on the top floor of the hotel. Their view was spectacular. The front of the room was all glass and they could see right across the oasis to the crystal fountain, sharply cut green maze, and the wildflowers that lay at the foot of the tropical forest. The mountainous walls of volcanic rock that ringed the crater and kept the world at bay were silhouetted against the sky.

Martine's first action had been to take a steaming hot bubble bath, and now she was lying pink-faced on one of the beds, swaddled in a gown so vast and fluffy it was like wearing a cloud. Their filthy clothes had been whisked away to the laundry.

"Don't you see that's exactly what he wants us to do?"

said Ben, who was wearing a red and blue striped robe several sizes too large for him. "He can't kidnap us because that's a serious offense and could ruin his chances of taking Sawubona. But if we walk out of here on our own, before it suits him, there's nothing to stop him calling the police and having us charged with breaking and entering, trespassing, and elephant assault . . ."

"*Assault?*" cried Martine. "I was trying to help Ruby. His pod workers were the ones who assaulted her."

"I know that and you know that, but it's our word against his. And frankly I don't think the police are going to be all that happy to find we're in Namibia with no passports and no guardians. After they're done with us, they'll probably charge Gwyn Thomas and my mum and dad with child neglect. The thing is, I don't believe Reuben James has any intention of harming us. He only wants us out of the way until Sawubona is safely in his hands."

Martine sat up. "I've just remembered something. When we were in the storage unit this morning I saw an entry on the delivery sheet for twenty vials of medicine. I couldn't remember what it was for at the time, but now I do. It's an animal tranquilizer."

Ben put down his knife and fork. "That bald man, Tony, he said that it was just as well it was only twenty-four hours until the elephants were gone, because they'd been cooped up so long they were ready to go on a rampage. If the hotel is due to open soon, it makes sense that Reuben James would want them gone. I bet you he's planning to ship them out to Sawubona tomorrow."

"Sawubona?" Martine pulled the gown more tightly around her. "Ben, we have to stop them. But how?"

"Well, right now what we really need to do is sleep. We're going to be no use to elephants or anyone else if we're half-dead with tiredness."

Martine wanted to disagree, but her brain was foggy with exhaustion and the words wouldn't come. "Okay," she said weakly, flopping down.

As the afternoon sun boiled down on Moon Valley, not a single bird sang.

Martine was awakened by a keycard clicking in the lock. Ben stirred at the same time and she heard him reach for the flashlight they'd left on the floor between them. He didn't turn it on, but Martine could sense him lying there in the darkness, poised to fight or flee.

The door opened briefly and a figure slipped into the room. Ben flicked the flashlight on. The intruder was the elephant whisperer. He blinked as the beam seared his pupils.

Martine's fear gave way to fury. "What do you think you're doing, Joseph? You nearly gave me a heart attack." But she softened once she saw that he was more frightened than she was.

"Forgive me for disturbing you, and for frightening you," he said. "I had to find a way to speak to you both alone. It has taken me up until now to find the key for your door. I beg you, please give me news of my son if you know anything at all. Although you denied it to Mr. James, I had the feeling that you'd met Gift or seen him."

Martine tried to harden her heart. "What do you care? According to Reuben James, you're here of your own free will. He says he has a deal with you to look after Gift if you look after the elephants. Obviously it doesn't matter to you that your son doesn't know whether you're dead or alive."

Joseph hung his head. "You are correct about the first thing. I have had the choice to walk out of here at any time and be reunited with my son. And in the beginning Mr. James would often offer to take me to him, provided, of course, that I never spoke of this place. He is not a wicked man. He genuinely believes in the Ark Project and the good that can come out of it. It is not him I am afraid of."

"Then who?" asked Ben.

Joseph lowered his voice. "His business partner, Callum. It's he who convinced Mr. James they should divert the stream in order to control all the water in Damaraland. Mr. James was very much against it but now he has agreed. I think Callum might have some kind of hold over him—perhaps to do with money. If they are allowed to succeed with this plan tomorrow, devastation will follow."

"I don't understand," said Martine. "You claim to love elephants, but you are helping these men with their sick experiments. You claim to love your son and say you're free to go, yet you are still here."

The elephant whisperer sank onto a chair and put his head in his hands. "Do you know the expression 'If you make your bed, you must lie on it'? A long time ago, I made a terrible decision. I'm afraid I have to live with the consequences."

"Everyone makes mistakes," Ben told him.

Joseph looked up. "Not like this. My elephants are family to me. They are like my brothers and sisters and uncles. Do you know what it's like to watch them die slowly in their hearts because the freedom of the desert winds has been taken from them; because they are confined? Elephants lose their minds in such a situation. They become so desperate to be free of captivity that they have been known to take their own lives. I thought I could help them endure this period with patience, play, and love, but I was wrong."

"You care for the elephants more than you care for your own son," accused Martine.

Joseph paled. "That is not true, and besides, it is not a competition. I love them all. Please don't judge me until you know the facts."

"We've been searching for the facts ever since we came to Namibia," Martine said a little sarcastically. "We'd love to know what they are."

A shudder went through Joseph. "One year ago, I had an argument with my son. I had noticed some changes in him since he started attending school in Windhoek and I felt they were not good ones. He was cocky. Cheeky. He had this notion to become a famous news photographer. To tell you the truth, I could not admit to him that I could no longer afford to pay for him to go to school, let alone college. I told him to get his head out of the clouds. He accused me of trying to take away his dream and destroy his future. He ran out of the house, threatening never to return.

"During the long night I searched for him, I had much time to think. I realized that I was a stubborn old fool, stuck in my ways, and that the world is changing. I saw that I was a fortunate man to have a son with a dream to become a photographer when so many of my friends have sons who are bone idle and want nothing more than to hang about the town, stealing and drinking and causing trouble. I vowed to do whatever it took to find the money to help him achieve his goals."

Martine and Ben were riveted. They sat side by side in their gowns and listened to the gentle man.

"Go on," Martine encouraged.

"Toward morning I was passing Moon Valley when Reuben James came by in his car. I have known him for many years and when he asked me what was wrong, I told him. After swearing me to secrecy, he brought me to Moon Valley and showed me the dome, which had just been completed. He told me of his ambition to create a super race of animals, ones that would survive global warming. He believed that this could be done by studying the desert elephants.

"He offered me more money than I had earned in my whole career to manage, train, and take care of the elephants and, when I hesitated, he doubled it."

"But the money came with a price attached?" guessed Ben.

Joseph nodded. "The Ark Project was top secret, which meant that if I wanted to be part of it I had to make a decision there and then. I could not even go home for one hour to explain everything to my son. I had to agree to cut off all contact with my former life for a period of twelve months. In return, Reuben said he would educate Gift and care for him as if he was his own son. He promised to do everything in his power to help him achieve his dream."

"So you signed on the dotted line," said Martine.

"I signed. The gates of Moon Valley closed and my life ended, all in the same moment."

Outside the hotel room, night had fallen. Martine listened for the crickets and frogs that made African nights so musical, but the crater was eerily still.

Ben made them coffee and they sat at the dining table drinking it. Joseph's story had made Martine worry again about Gift and why he'd never returned to the Welcome Center. There was a catch in her voice as she said, "If it's any consolation, Reuben James has at least honored his promise about Gift."

Over the next half hour, she and Ben told Joseph every detail of the days they'd spent with Gift, starting with him rescuing them in the red dunes of Sossusvlei and ending with him dropping them off at the Stone Age etchings in Damaraland. Neither of them said anything about Gift failing to reappear and their concerns that something might have happened to him. Rather, they put the blame on themselves, saying they'd wandered off and gotten lost in the desert.

Seldom had Martine seen a man so transformed by a piece of news. It was as if they'd given Joseph a tonic. He looked twenty years younger.

"The way my son helped you makes me proud," he said. "And this photography career you say he has and the home he has built, these are the best things a father could hear. Knowing that my boy has become a man and, not only that, a gentleman, these words are like the sunshine to me."

He stood up. "I am already in your debt and we don't have much time, but I wonder if I can be permitted to ask you one more question."

"Go ahead," said Ben with a smile.

"I heard you talking to Mr. James about the elephant that was tortured and tormented by Lurk. You said she was living at Sawubona? Sawubona is your home in South Africa?"

"It is," said Martine. "It's a game reserve near Storm Crossing. My grandfather and our game warden, Tendai, took Angel in and made her well again. She's happy now, I think, but she always seems lonely."

She decided not to mention that, barring a miracle, in three days' time Sawubona would be taken over by Reuben James and Angel would belong to him. So, agonizingly, would the white giraffe.

"That is good to hear. They had sent her away a long time before I was brought to this place, but as soon as the other workers described her I knew they were talking of one of my favorite elephants—one I knew for over thirty years. I was heartbroken, imagining the worst. My comfort here has been the companionship of her sister."

Martine stared at him as if he'd grown wings. "Her *sister!*"

Joseph nodded. "Ruby, the elephant you healed today. She is the twin sister of your Angel."

He turned to leave.

"I'm confused, Joseph," said Ben. You signed up to be at Moon Valley for twelve months. That means you must be due to go home to Gift any day now?"

The elephant whisperer looked down. "I have reached the end of my contract, yes, but there is a problem."

"I don't suppose it has anything to do with Callum?" said Martine.

Joseph reacted as if she'd poked him with a burning stick. "Please, Miss Martine, keep your voice down. A few months ago, Callum warned me that if I walked away from the Ark Project, I must do so knowing that one day—it could be tomorrow or in ten years—Gift would meet with an accident. I hope it is his idea of a joke, but I am afraid to test him. If it is a choice between my life and my son's, I will choose to save Gift's, even if it means he must grow up without a father."

There was a knock at the door. They almost jumped out of their skins.

"What if that's him?" Joseph fretted. "He must not find me here. He'll think I've been telling you secrets."

"Hide in the closet," said Martine. "Don't worry. Whatever happens, we'll protect you."

The knock came again, louder this time.

Ben bounced up and went to the door. "Can I help you?" he mumbled in a polite but sleepy voice.

"Housekeeping."

He opened up cautiously, scared it might be a trap. A smiling maid handed him a parcel. It was their ragged clothes, washed and ironed.

"Good evening," she said. "I am here with your laundry and a message from Reuben James. He sent me to ask if you would like some dinner."

29

They were ready to go before first light. They'd done all they could to persuade Joseph to come with them, but he wouldn't leave his elephants. If his elephant family was going to be moved, he wanted to be with them. And he refused to do anything that might endanger his son.

After making Martine and Ben promise that they wouldn't reveal his location to a living soul, he gave them an elephant hair bracelet and said, "If you see Gift, find some way to put this in his possessions so that he will come across it one day and know that I am alive and I love him."

"No," said Martine. "You're going to give it to him yourself."

Despite that, the elephant whisperer had agreed to tell them the code that opened the main gate, and the time the guards took their morning tea. He confessed that he'd memorized everything because he'd dreamed so often of escape, or of sneaking out to see Gift.

Outside, the morning air was bracingly cold and the wooden walkways were slippery with dew. Martine rubbed her arms to try to generate some warmth as they crept through the still, quiet forest. She'd never realized that a world without birdsong could be so spooky or lonely or empty. She didn't blame the local people for not wanting to come here.

The sky was mauve above the black ring of volcanic rock as they neared the main gate. The guards were still there, but at 5:15 on the dot they disappeared into their guardhouse for tea, as Joseph had promised.

"This seems too easy. I keep expecting something to go wrong," Martine whispered as Ben typed the code into the keypad next to the gate.

"It should be easy," he said. "We're not supposed to be prisoners, remember."

But the words were barely out of his mouth when Reuben James came running up. He was out of breath and unshaven and his clothes were disheveled, as if he'd been roused from sleep and dressed in a hurry.

The gate clicked open. Standing on the other side, poised to ring the bell, were Lurk and Callum.

Lurk's eyes bulged. He lifted a finger and pointed. "Maxine!"

As Callum stepped through the gate, the security men emerged from the guardhouse with crumbs on their faces, stammering excuses.

"What are you up to now, Reuben?" Callum said. "Thought you'd give the local schoolkids a guided tour at the crack of dawn, did you?"

His black eyes flickered over Martine like a lizard's tongue. Up close, his chilly smile, blue-black crow's feather hair, and thick black brows gave him the appearance of a movie hit man. Martine had never met anyone she could truly have described as evil before, but this man fit the bill.

"Martine and Ben, meet my business partner, Callum," said Reuben James, rattled but doing his best not to show it. "Lurk you already know. Callum, you're earlier than expected, but it's not a problem. I'll wake the chef and organize you some breakfast."

Martine noticed that he didn't answer Callum's question. Callum must have noticed it too, because his gaze slid over to Martine, then Ben, and then back to Martine again.

He said silkily, "Have we met before?"

"I tole you she was not Anna," Lurk said, glaring at Martine over Callum's shoulder. "I tole you she was the one who made the elephant to chase me."

Reuben James said, "Shut up, Lurk. Of course you haven't met her, Callum. She and her friend are not from Namibia. Don't worry, they're just leaving."

Callum continued to scrutinize Martine. "You're the girl from the game reserve in South Africa, aren't you? I've seen a newspaper photo of you and your white giraffe. For some reason, that rings alarm bells for me. I'm wondering what you might be doing at Moon Valley, which is a top secret project. Could someone enlighten me?"

"I was showing them around the hotel and they know not to tell anyone about it," said Reuben James. "They're good kids and they've done nothing wrong, Callum. Come on, Martine and Ben, I'll take you home."

Callum smiled his evil smile. "What's the hurry, Reuben? Surely Martine and Ben would like some breakfast too. Maybe they'd also like to know what you have planned for their game reserve in South Africa?"

Reuben James froze. "What are you playing at, Callum?"

Callum put an arm around the other man's shoulders. "I'm wondering the same thing about you, my friend. Why don't we take a little walk to the pod and see what's going on there? Oh, and Reuben, I wouldn't bother trying to persuade the guards to have me removed from Moon Valley. Like Lurk, they're all in my pay, and, as the old saying goes, the piper calls the tune."

A hush came over the dome when the door crashed open. The pod workers, who were stuffing elephant toys into boxes and dismantling laboratory equipment, halted where they were like freeze-framed figures in a film. Anything moveable had been cleared away, including the elephants, who were assembled in their shackles on the far side of the dome. Joseph was struggling to get them in order. As soon as he had them quieted, he stopped what he was doing and turned around.

"Is it spring-cleaning day or are you and your workers

going somewhere, Reuben?" asked Callum. He nodded to the men in white coats. "Gentlemen, would you leave us." They scuttled out without a word.

It was cold in the dome but Martine noticed diamonds of sweat had broken out on Reuben James's forehead. He cleared his throat. "Callum, I told you that we were preparing to move the elephants to Sawubona today."

"You don't have the right to do that," cried Martine. "It's *our* game reserve and my grandmother is in England right now making sure that you never get your hands on it."

Callum raised his eyebrows. "*Your* game reserve. Not for much longer, I'm afraid. You know the old Bible story about the Great Flood and Noah saving the animals by taking them two by two onto his ark. Well, Reuben plans to breed global-warming-resistant animals on *our* game reserve using the genes of species like the desert elephants and Oryx, who can live on a fraction of the food and water of ordinary wildlife. Hence the name: the *Ark* Project."

"Nothing wrong with preparing animals for the future," Reuben James said defensively. "I'm doing my best to learn how to save them. It's conservation."

Martine felt a chill go through her. "That depends on how you go about it."

Callum laughed. "Isn't it obvious? You conduct experiments with the most unique and rare animals, animals with special powers, animals such as the white giraffe."

"No!" cried Martine.

"It won't be like that, Callum," Reuben James said furiously.

"It will when I take over Sawubona. Or maybe I'll just auction the animals off to the highest bidder. The white giraffe alone should fetch a cool million. You haven't forgotten, have you, Reuben, how much you are in my debt. If you don't start remembering who's boss around here, there'll come a day when everything you own will be mine."

Reuben James curled his lip. "I'm finished with this, Callum. I want nothing more to do with you and your spy." He glared pointedly at Lurk. "I convinced myself that by diverting the stream, we'd be doing more good for the people and animals of Damaraland than bad. Now I realize that you poison everything you touch. That you care nothing for anyone but yourself. I'll have my lawyer contact yours to draw up some repayment plan with the money. Come, Martine and Ben, let's go. I'm sorry you had to see this."

Startled at this turn of events, Martine and Ben moved to follow him, but Lurk and Nipper barred their way.

"I don't think so," said Callum.

Reuben James gave a harsh laugh. "How are you planning to stop us? Are you going to kill us?"

On the other side of the dome, Martine saw Joseph go rigid. She tried to catch his eye, but he turned away and began fussing over Ruby.

Callum flashed his business partner a smile. "You've been reading too much fiction, my friend. Of course I'm not going to kill you. Not only would that would be bad for my reputation as a businessman, it's messy and unnecessary. I mean, we have a whole desert on our doorstep. Terrible things, deserts. Even the most experienced men could run out of petrol in the middle of nowhere on the very day that they've forgotten their water bottles. They could easily perish from heatstroke. It could be years before their bones are found. Elephant whisperers and small children can run into the same sort of trouble. It's a shame, but these things happen.

"Oh, and don't worry about the elephants. They're very valuable dead or alive. I'll take very good care of them."

"You monster," said Reuben James in a barely audible voice. Lurk and the two guards closed in on him.

"Right, Nipper," Callum said, "time to get on with the business of the day. Are you ready with the dynamite?"

Nipper saluted.

"In some ways it's a relief that you'll be out of the picture, Reuben," Callum said. "It means a bigger piece of the pie for me. In a few minutes' time, we're going to blast the final wall that holds back the spring and then we will control all the water in Damaraland. Next I'll move on to a project in the red dunes of Sossusvlei and do the same there, and pretty soon I'll own all the water in Namibia. I'll be able to charge what I like for it."

A shrill whistle cut short his speech. Everyone turned to look at Joseph in surprise. His right arm was raised. He dropped it and the elephants cast off their shackles and charged, many of them trumpeting along the way. It was like some centuries-old army tearing into battle, blowing their bugles.

Martine grabbed hold of Ben, convinced they were about to be trampled to death, but the first elephant to reach them was Ruby. She encircled them both with her trunk and stood over them protectively.

Elsewhere in the dome it was pure chaos. There were swinging tusks and yelling men everywhere. Lurk was tossed about like an elephant's football, and Callum Murphy, Reuben James, and the guards disappeared inside an elephant scrum.

Joseph hurried over to Martine. "Go now," he said. "Nobody will stop you."

"Come with us," pleaded Ben.

Joseph smiled. "I'll be right behind you. First, I must take care of my elephants. For twelve long months, they have taken care of me."

They tore through the door and down the hill to the main gate. Ben typed in the code. "Forty-eight hours," he said to Martine. "We have forty-eight hours to save Sawubona."

The gate clicked open and they stepped dazed into the morning. Ringed around the construction site were a dozen police cars, some with rifles trained out of the windows. Before they could react, the rifles lowered. The door of one of the cars opened and out jumped their friend. He was positively beaming.

Ben grinned. "We're in luck. Gift's brought the cavalry."

"About time too," said Martine. "Hey, Ben, look."

A line of elephants was streaming down the hill with Joseph at its head, but something even more incredible had caught Martine's attention. A lilac-breasted roller bird had settled on the roof of the guardhouse and it was trilling its heart out.

30

They flew back to South Africa first class next morning, courtesy of the Namibian government, who had agreed to "turn a blind eye" to their lack of passports.

"It's the least we could do," a government official told Ben and Martine as a delegation bearing treats such as Black Forest gateaux and Nara melons saw them off at the airport in Windhoek. "If these men had been allowed to carry out their fiendish plan, our most precious resource might have been destroyed, bringing ruin and devastation to vast areas of our country."

The environment minister had been so overjoyed that twenty rare desert elephants, thought to be dead, had been saved that he'd offered Martine and Ben a free holiday in Namibia with their families as a thank you. They'd asked if they could have Ruby instead. He was bewildered by their request until Joseph explained that Ruby was related to their own desert elephant, Angel, at which point he agreed at once. Unlike Martine and Ben, Ruby was going to be traveling to Sawubona by road, and would be reunited with her twin on Christmas Day.

For Martine and Ben, landing amid the crowds and

buzz of Cape Town airport was a shock to the system after the space and silence of the desert. The first thing they saw was a newsstand. Gift's striking photographs of Reuben James in handcuffs and Callum and Lurk being lifted into an ambulance on stretchers were prominently displayed on several front pages. The *Cape Times* also carried his picture of his father, Joseph, leading the elephants to safety.

Martine bought a couple of papers with her remaining change and tucked them into her bag to read later. She smiled at the thought that Gift was already well on his way to achieving his dream of becoming a news photographer—an achievement made all the more special because he could now share it with his dad. There hadn't been many dry eyes after their reunion. They'd promised to visit Martine and Ben at Sawubona in the new year. Martine hadn't been able to find the words to tell them that she and Ben might not be on the game reserve by then. Following Reuben James's arrest, the future of Sawubona was more uncertain than ever.

Tendai was waiting in the arrivals hall to greet them. He shook hands formally with Ben and swept Martine off her feet, his booming laughter attracting stares.

"There's nothing left of you, little one," he scolded. "Grace is going to have something to say about that. What have you been eating for the past week?"

"Oh, Nara melons and hoodia cacti mainly," said Martine as they walked out to the parking lot. "Plus a few croissants. How is Grace?"

Tendai rolled his eyes. "That impossible woman! After you and Ben went missing, I wanted to call the police, but she admitted that she'd read the bones and told you to go as far as you needed to in order to pluck out the thorn that was hurting you. I told her she had finally lost her mind. I was so angry I didn't speak to her for a week. I have had sleepless nights thinking of the many ways your grandmother would punish me for allowing you out of my sight."

He opened the jeep door and Martine and Ben climbed in.

"I'm sorry for worrying you, Tendai," said Martine, "but you know, Grace was right about everything. The circle did lead us to the elephants."

Tendai started the engine. "She always is."

"My grandmother?" Martine said, plucking up the courage to ask the question she'd been dreading hearing the answer to. "Has she called from England? Does she know we were missing?"

"She doesn't, because after you went my aunt Grace persuaded the wife of one of the guards, a hotel receptionist, to record an answer machine message saying there was a fault on the line." He held up a palm. "I want you to know that I had no part in this."

Martine tried to keep a straight face. "I'm sure you didn't."

"As a result, your poor grandmother has not been able to reach the house at all. Grace picked up the phone for the first time this morning, after we heard you were coming back. Your grandmother was on a pay phone. All she had time to say was that she is flying into Cape Town tomorrow morning, on Christmas Eve, and that she has good news."

They saved their story till they got back to Sawubona, and even then it had to wait because, although Martine paused to thank Grace and be smothered in the *sangoma's* warm embrace, she could not wait another minute to see Jemmy.

The white giraffe and Angel were standing by the game park gate, almost as if they'd known she was coming. The elephant retreated shyly when Martine walked up. Her gaze was fixed on the road and Martine wondered if she'd sensed, or heard, that her twin was on her way. Gift had told her elephants could communicate across distances as far as six miles, using low-frequency calls that could be heard, or felt and interpreted by their trunks and sensitive feet, but it was a stretch to believe they communicate between countries.

Still, they were supremely evolved beings—far smarter than people, in Martine's opinion—so anything was possible.

"Ruby will be here in two days' time," she said to Angel. "You'll be together on Christmas Day." Under her breath she added: "I only hope that I'm here too."

The white giraffe put his head down and she threw her arms around his neck and pressed her face to his silken silver muzzle, as she'd longed to do so often during her desert ordeal. "I'm so sorry I left you, Jemmy. If it was up to me I wouldn't be away from you for a minute, not even to go to school, but you can't believe the messes grown-ups get themselves into, or the trouble they cause. And Ben and I keep getting caught in the middle."

She kissed him. "If it's any consolation, thinking about you kept me strong. When you told me you loved me, that's what got me through."

She didn't add: "And that's what's going to get us through the next twenty-four hours until we know whether or not we've done enough to save Sawubona."

Grace and Tendai eventually got to hear the elephants' tale—for that, Martine and Ben were agreed, was what it was—over coffee and chocolate cake.

They told the story jointly, with lots of interruptions. Martine started by describing how they'd stowed away on Reuben James's plane and had been stranded in the desert.

Tendai was aghast. "What were the two of you thinking? *Anything* could have happened to you. When your grand-mother gets back from England, Martine, she will fire me for sure. No wonder I am a nervous wreck."

"Tendai, you have nerves like a girl," Grace told him rudely. "Now go on, honey. How did ya find the circle?"

Martine continued, explaining how they'd ended up at Moon Valley and about Gift's dramatic reappearance. It turned out that the text he'd received about his camera lens had been a hoax. When he reached Hoodia Lodge,

Lurk had tricked him into a storage cellar and locked him up for the night as revenge for the gift shop humiliation.

Rummaging through boxes in an attempt to find a tool that might help him escape, Gift had come across files on the tests carried out on the missing elephants. That's when he realized that Martine and Ben had been onto something. He'd smashed the lock on the door and rushed to call the police.

"If it wasn't for the white giraffe, I don't know if we'd have found you," Gift had told them. "It would never have occurred to me that you'd been mad enough or brave enough to walk miles across the desert in the dead of night, sneak into a heavily secured extinct volcano, and start causing havoc."

In the kitchen at Sawubona, Tendai spooned condensed milk into his tea. He'd pulled himself together since being told off by his aunt, but his hand still shook. "So the elephant whisperer saved you by getting the elephants to stampede?"

"Joseph blew the whistle that started it, but the elephants came up with the plan to pretend they were still shackled on their own," Martine told him. "Tendai, you can't believe how sensitive and intelligent and incredible they are. Their hearts break when they are separated from their loved ones or trapped in captivity. When Ruby collapsed, I think they decided that they'd had enough. They were so desperate for freedom they were prepared to die rather than be tormented any longer."

Ben said, "Well, they definitely got their own back. The paramedic I talked to told me that Callum was going to be in hospital for at least three months and one of the detectives said he was pretty sure the courts would lock the man up and throw away the key. The ambulance guy also told me that Lurk would be spending a lot of time in the hospital before he went to jail as well. Apparently he has a string of previous convictions for burglary, assault, and other crimes."

"Do you think it was him who broke into your grandmother's office?" Tendai asked, shocked.

"The Namibian police thought it was highly likely," answered Martine. "He was Reuben James's chauffeur, but he was paid by Callum to spy on his boss. Their guess is that when Reuben began getting cold feet about the Ark Project, Callum sent Lurk to try to find some documents that would help them steal Sawubona from under him if necessary."

"What are your feelings about Reuben James now?" Tendai wanted to know. "Did you change your mind about him after he turned against Callum and stood up for you?"

It was a question Martine and Ben found difficult to answer. Was Reuben James as corrupt as his business partner? Or was he a well-intentioned man who'd genuinely wanted to save animals and water but had been blackmailed into doing the wrong thing? In return for not going to jail, he'd promised to sell all his Namibian hotels and, after the debts were cleared, donate half the profits to global warming and elephant charities. He was also going to set up a trust fund for Gift, in an attempt to make up for the time the boy had spent without his father.

"I guess we'll know if he's nice or nasty tomorrow when we find out whether he's still planning to take our home," said Martine. "Oh, I hope so much that my grandmother's good news is about the game reserve. Keeping Sawubona and Jemmy and Khan would be the best Christmas present I could ever wish for."

After the meal, Ben went out with Tendai to check on the game reserve and Martine helped Grace do the dishes. Standing at the sink, up to her elbows in warm soapy suds, Martine found that the whole Namibian adventure had already taken on a dreamlike quality.

"You're very quiet, chile," said Grace. "Was I right to tell ya to go as far as ya needed to go to find truth?"

Martine dried her hands and put an arm around the *sangoma's* ample waist. "Yes, you did the right thing. I'm proud if Ben and I played some part in freeing the elephants, but . . ."

"But what?"

"It's nothing really."

"It ain't nothin' if it make you feel blue. It ain't nothin' if the thorn is still in your heart."

"It's just . . ."

"Go on."

"Well, it's just that when you told me that the elephants would lead me to the truth, I thought you meant that I'd find out the truth behind my gift. I suppose I'm a bit sad that I'm no wiser."

Grace smiled. "The four leaves led you to the circle, didn't they? And the circle led you to the elephants, right?"

"Right."

"Where did the elephants lead you?"

Martine thought about it for a second. "The elephants led me back here. They led me . . . they led me to Sawubona."

She took a step back. "What are you saying, Grace? That the truth is here? You know it, don't you? You know my story."

Grace pulled out a chair and sat down. Her face gave nothing away. "I know a little."

Through the kitchen window, Martine saw Jemmy. He was still at the gate; still waiting for her. At the sight of the white giraffe, the frustration that had been building in her for months suddenly bubbled up and spilled over. It was driving her crazy that she'd been given a gift and yet she didn't really know what it was for, or why she'd been given it in the first place. It was almost cruel.

"Why would the ancestors choose me?" she said emotionally to Grace. "It doesn't make any sense and in some ways it feels wrong. Although I was born at Sawubona, I grew up in England, so I'm more British than South African. Plus I'm a white girl and dead ordinary. Why didn't they choose an African child—someone special like Gift, for example?"

"The ancestors didn't choose you. You chose yourself."

Martine sat down slowly. "What do you mean?"

"I mean, chile, that the gift is not to do with skin color or place of birth. It ain't nothin' to do with ordinary or extraordinary. It's to do with love."

Grace took a sip of tea. "Take your elephant whisperer friend. You tell me he were snatched by an elephant during a raid, and that he was found a couple a months later, living happy as can be with the herd. A million other boys, they woulda been crushed by these same elephants. But Joseph, he had a pure love in his heart for these elephants and they knew he spoke their language."

Martine felt tears spring into her eyes. That's how she'd felt the moment she encountered Jemmy. She'd known then that he was her soul mate and that she'd go to the ends of the earth, as she'd done in the past few weeks, to love him and keep him safe. It was agony not knowing if she and Ben had done enough.

"Same with you, chile," Grace went on. "Every generation has its healers—some for people, some for animals. A thousand eleven-year-old children coulda looked out their window one stormy night, as you did, and seen the white giraffe. Most woulda been excited and a few mighta been bold enough to go into the game reserve, like you, ta take a closer look. But only one of those children would have cared enough, been patient enough, and loved enough to tame the white giraffe.

"The forefathers, the ancestors, they predicted that a white giraffe would be born on this here piece of land; that it would be orphaned and rescued by an elephant and find sanctuary in the Secret Valley. They saw that only the unconditional love of a chile could heal this creature and that, in turn, the white giraffe would give something back—a power to heal other animals."

"But they didn't know it would be me?" said Martine softly.

"No, they didn't know it would be you." Grace put a hand on her shoulder. "But I did, chile. I did."

Martine's heart was pounding as if she'd run a marathon. Outside, she could hear the peaceful crooning of doves. She wondered if they'd sound so content if Reuben James took over Sawubona, or whether he'd have speakers dotted around the garden again, booming out birdsong.

She covered Grace's brown hand with her pale one. "Thank you for telling me what you know about my gift. It helps. I've been feeling guilty about it. I've been thinking, 'Why me? I've done nothing to deserve this.' But now that I know it's about love, I'm not so scared of it. I feel lighter somehow. Maybe there's something in that saying about how the truth can set you free."

"Sure is," said Grace heartily. "Sure is."

"Grace, I've faced quite a lot of challenges in the year I've been at Sawubona, haven't I?"

"Sure have, honey. And you've come out of them stronger."

Martine smiled. "Does that mean I now have the eyes and the experience to read the meaning behind the paintings in the Memory Room?"

The *sangoma* gave her a squeeze. "Why don't ya go there and find out."

"Really? Can I go tonight? Grace, do you think it would it be okay if I showed Ben the Secret Valley? We've shared so much together."

"Of course. Like I tol' you: He's part of your story."

31

The thing Ben couldn't get over was how smooth and rhythmic Jemmy's stride was. "It's like riding a flying carpet!" he told Martine as they galloped across the moonlit savannah, past a pride of watchful lions and a herd of skittish springbok.

Martine was in her element because she'd never had the chance to share the experience of racing the white giraffe with anyone (she and Grace had proceeded across the game reserve at a sloth-like pace), and never thought she would. Her grandmother wouldn't have approved, but the way Martine saw it, riding Jemmy across Sawubona by the light of a full moon, with Ben accompanying her for added protection, was a lot safer than stowing away on planes, or being stranded in foreign deserts with megalomaniacs and marauding elephants.

When they reached the barren clearing and the twisted tree that guarded the Secret Valley, Ben was incredulous. "I've passed this place a hundred times with Tendai, and would never have guessed there was anything here. It's always seemed so desolate."

"Shut your eyes and hold on tight," ordered Martine. She gripped hard with her calves and grabbed a fistful of silver mane. Jemmy's quarters bunched and then they were crashing through the thorny creeper and the invisible space between the shelves of rock behind.

"It would be great if my mum and dad don't return from their cruise to find me in full traction in a hospital bed," Ben said, clinging white-knuckled to Martine as the white giraffe came to a snorting, shuddering halt. "Am I allowed to open my eyes yet? What is this place anyway? It has a wonderful perfume."

"That's from the orchids. Ben, do you trust me?"

"I'd trust you with my life."

"Then keep your eyes closed a while longer. Down, Jemmy, there's a good boy."

The white giraffe's knees buckled and he sank to the ground. Martine helped Ben to dismount. She took his hand and led him along the twisting tunnel, keeping hopeful watch for Khan, up the mossy steps, through the bat antechamber, and into the Memory Room.

"All right," she said. "You can look now."

Ben opened his eyes and stared, dazzled by the paintings. Their ancient hues were so fiery and vivid they seemed to dance across the rock walls.

Martine giggled at her friend's incredulous expression.

"Martine, this is the most magical place I've ever been to. It's like your own private art gallery."

Martine sat down on the cool stone bench. "That's how I always feel. It's my favorite place on earth and I can't believe we're here. There were so many times in the desert when I didn't think we'd make it."

Ben sat down beside her. "Same here. But this place makes everything worth it. Hey, what's that? It looks a bit like an elephant footprint."

Martine stared. He was pointing at the patch that she had asked Grace about, the splotch she'd considered a mistake. Looking at it from a distance, she saw that it was indeed an elephant footprint. She noticed something else too. It occupied a single, hexagonal cell in a faintly drawn honeycomb structure. All of the other cells were empty, apart from one, which contained a series of miniature symbols. Martine couldn't begin to think how to interpret them.

Out in the antechamber, the bats started squeaking wildly. Through the cave entrance, they could see a black whirlwind of them. Ben leaped to his feet. "Could someone be coming?"

"Only Khan," said Martine, but when the leopard didn't appear, unease began to gnaw at her. "Nobody else knows about this place except Grace and me."

Ben settled down again, but she could tell that he was jumpy. To get his attention she said, "I've got an idea."

Ben groaned. "Whenever you have an idea, it seems to involve illegal activities and saber-toothed wild animals."

"No, this is easy. All we have to do is lie on our backs in different parts of the cave and look at the ceiling."

"What's the catch?"

Martine gave him a playful shove. "There is none, silly. It's an experiment, that's all."

They lay on their backs on the cold stone, gazing up at the roof of the cave.

"Well, this is fun," said Ben. "Can we do it again sometime?"

Martine couldn't help giggling. "Tell me what you see."

"I see a lot of rock." He wriggled to another section of the cave. "Oh, and there's more rock. Hold on, I think I can see . . . yes, it's definitely rock!"

He was moving once again when Martine let out a yelp of excitement. "Ben, come over here. The roof of the cave. Can you see? It's shaped like a hexagon."

Two minutes later, they were in the labyrinth of tunnels Grace had led Martine through on the night they'd found the elephant tusks. As they walked, Ben left a trail of crumbs from the rusks they'd brought to snack on, so they could find their way out again. "Like Hansel and Gretel in the fairy tale," he said with a laugh.

They soon found that Martine's theory was correct. Through some quirk of geology, every cave was hexagon-shaped. Some were more lopsided than others, but basically the Secret Valley was a giant honeycomb. If the Memory Room was, as Martine suspected, the cave indicated by the elephant's footprint, then the cave with the symbols would be the one farthest from the valley entrance.

Deeper and deeper they went under the mountain, their flashlight beams piercing the darkness. The structure of the walls around them deteriorated as they went. Soon the slightest brush of the wall produced a trickle of granite powder, and the evidence of rock falls became more frequent. Each new cave was dustier and more cobweb-strewn than the last.

Once, Martine thought she heard footsteps. The hairs stood up on the back of her neck. "Do you think there are ghosts in here?"

"Probably," Ben said, "but it's more likely we're hearing bats or *dassies*. I reckon we should turn back. If the tunnel collapses, we'll be buried alive."

"Please, Ben, we only have one cave to go."

Knowing how much it meant to her, he relented. "One more cave and then we're going back even if I have to carry you."

The air was stale and musty and laden with dust. It was like breathing in old cobwebs. The roof of the tunnel was not much higher than their heads. Part of Martine wanted to run away screaming, but something stronger than herself seemed to be pulling her forward, almost dragging her.

At last the cave was before them. It was the smallest so far and the most damaged. Pyramids of broken rock were heaped about the floor. Spiders scuttled from webs as thick as net curtains.

"There's nothing here," Martine said in disappointment. "If there were symbols or paintings here once, they've long since faded. Let's go."

"Hold on a second." Ben shone the flashlight at the cave roof. "Do you notice something? It's not hexagonal."

Martine was more concerned with the trickle of dirt falling from a hole above her. Was it her imagination or was it getting faster? "Ben, I think we should get out of here. The roof looks as if it's about to come down on our heads."

"All right, but give me one second. I want to look at something." He moved toward the far wall. There was a blood-curdling roar and Khan sprang from the shadows. His massive paws thudded into Ben's chest, throwing the boy to the ground.

"Khan!" screamed Martine. "No!"

There was a crack like a rifle shot and a slab of rock fell from the ceiling, landing where Ben had been standing a moment before. Rocks rained down as the roof of the cave began to crumble.

Martine ran to Ben's side and they crouched on the floor with Khan, covering their heads with their arms as shale showered down on them. There was nowhere to run. One side of the cave was breaking away. It seemed certain that they'd be entombed with the spiders and bats. All Martine could think about was Jemmy and how much she wished she'd had a chance to say good-bye to him.

Gradually, the rockslide slowed. The dust it left behind clogged their lungs and coated their mouths. Coughing, Martine picked up the flashlight and climbed shakily to her feet. Dirt cascaded from her clothes and hair. She rubbed her eyes, trying to clear the grit from them.

Behind the fallen wall was another cave. Khan walked forward and Martine followed. Ben hung back, watching as Martine and the leopard stopped and gazed about them. He could see that the walls of the cave were covered in faded paintings, strewn with spiderwebs, but something told him that Martine could see far more. He turned away, not wanting to intrude.

Only time and experience will give you the eyes to understand them, Grace had always told Martine about the cave paintings. And now, finally, she did. Her life's journey unfolded before her, just as Grace had always predicted it would.

She squatted down with her arm around the leopard, and saw her destiny unfold in the faded sketches as clearly as if she was watching a movie. Every image involved animals—jungle gorillas fleeing poachers, tigers caught in snares, polar bears on melting ice caps, or whales escaping the ships of hunters. And in every scene a boy and girl were helping them.

There was a low rumble. Khan snarled. He nipped at Martine's ankle. A thunderous roar blasted her eardrums and then the rest of the roof gave way.

"Run!" yelled Ben. He grabbed Martine's hand and the two of them flew into the tunnel. The leopard raced past them. Martine and Ben tore after him, trusting he knew the way. The crumbs were no use to them now.

The noise was deafening. The tunnel collapsed behind them as they ran, throwing forward stinging shards of rock and a steam-train plume of dust. Martine was starting to despair of ever getting out alive, when the starry sky that lit the mountainside exit came into view. Coughing and choking, she stumbled into the open air. She sank to the ground and gulped in oxygen. The leopard came over to her and licked her face with a tongue like sandpaper.

"Thanks, Khan," Martine said, half laughing, half sobbing. "You saved our lives."

Ben put a cautious hand out to stroke the leopard. "He saved mine twice."

Dawn was breaking when they reached the bottom of the mountain, where Jemmy was waiting, pacing up and down in a state of agitation. He'd heard the terrifying roar of the collapsing catacomb and had been almost out of his mind with fear because he couldn't get to Martine. They were amused to see that a friend had come to comfort him.

"Looks like you have a ride home, Ben," Martine said, her tongue firmly in her cheek.

"Oh, no," protested Ben. "You're not getting me up there. The last time I saw that elephant, she was hurtling after Lurk and trying to trample him to death."

"That was out of character," said Martine with a grin. "You'll be fine. Angel by name, Angel by nature."

32

Gwyn Thomas arrived home on the morning of Christmas Eve. By then, Ben and Martine were showered, scrubbed, and in their best jeans and shirts, which wasn't saying much, but it impressed the returning traveler. She was so thrilled to see them that she forgot, for once, to be reserved. She threw her arms around them and was quite overcome.

"I'm so thankful to be back at Sawubona, a herd of stampeding elephants couldn't drag me away," she said. Martine had to restrain herself from adding: "You'd be surprised what a herd of stampeding elephants can do."

They led her into the kitchen, where the table was spread with one of Grace's finest brunches—a meal of sliced paw paw and mango, jungle oats, farm eggs, wild mushrooms, roasted tomatoes, and great slabs of homemade seed bread. Martine marveled that Grace had managed to find the time get to the local farm store with everything else that had been going on.

"What a welcome," said Gwyn Thomas, visibly moved. "And what a picture of domestic bliss. When I couldn't get through on the phone, I was imagining all kinds of mayhem going on at Sawubona. I was worried sick that the two of you"—she nodded toward Ben and Martine—"were getting into all sorts of trouble in an attempt to save our home and animals. Obviously my sleepless nights were for nothing. You've looked after the game reserve and each other beautifully."

Martine realized she was holding her breath. "The deadline for us to move out of Sawubona is midnight tonight, but you told Grace when you called that you had some good news. Please tell me that I'm not going to be taken away from Jemmy. Please tell me that everything is going to be okay."

Her grandmother smiled. "Everything *is* going to be okay, but it's taken some doing. You wouldn't believe what I've been through. At times I've felt like a character in a thriller."

Grace handed her a glass of fresh orange juice and took her place at the table. She winked at Ben and Martine. "Why don't ya tell us all about it, honey?" she said.

Gwyn Thomas had been getting nowhere fast in England until she learned that the solicitor who'd drawn up the will produced by Reuben James had been sacked from Cutter & Buck, and was facing fraud charges.

"He was on bail, pending trial, and was quite aggressive with me," she explained, "but I soon had him remembering his manners."

Martine smiled to herself at the thought of this hardened fraudster being reduced to quivering jelly by her grandmother.

"After a series of quite extraordinarily creative lies and excuses, he admitted that Henry had been to see him at Cutter and Buck the summer before he died and had paid back all the money he owed Reuben James. That very morning, however, this solicitor had overheard Mr. James saying that he would do anything to get his hands on Sawubona. He saw an opportunity to make a fast buck. Unknown to my dear husband, he placed a new copy of the will beneath the paper that acknowledged receipt of the money. Henry signed it without knowing that he was in fact signing away the game reserve."

"What a devious, treacherous man this solicitor is," said Tendai, appalled.

"That was my opinion. His plan was to extract money from Reuben James for helping him to get Sawubona. He claims that Reuben wanted nothing to do with it at first and even threatened to get him sacked, but that as his debts mounted and he became obsessed with some animal project he had planned for the game reserve, his business partner pressured him to go along with it."

She smiled. "The good news I have to share with you is that Reuben James, in an apparent attack of remorse, contacted my solicitor yesterday and said he is withdrawing any claim to the game reserve. Our home is safe and so are our animals and the jobs of our staff."

They all cheered and clinked mugs. It was the best Christmas present any of them could wish for.

"What about the key?" asked Martine. "Did you ever find out what it was for?"

"Quite by chance I did," said Gwyn Thomas. "I went to visit your old Hampshire neighbors, the Morrisons, and Mrs. Morrison reminded me that she'd written to me not long after the fire to say that Veronica had given her a suitcase for safekeeping and did I want her to send it. I had so many other things to think about at the time that it went clean out of my mind."

"What was in the suitcase?" Ben said curiously.

"Documents mainly. Research on global warming, elephants, and something called the Ark Project. I always believed that Veronica wrote about nothing but sponge cakes and sofa upholstery, but it turns out that Henry had told her the story about our elephant Angel, who came to us from some dreadful Namibian zoo, and she was looking into it before she died. I passed all her files over to a detective at Scotland Yard."

She paused to spread gooseberry jam on her toast. "I didn't think anything would come of it, but right before I boarded the plane for Cape Town, he called my cell phone. He said something about Mr. James being arrested in Namibia for abducting elephants and trying to start a water war. It was most peculiar. I think I must have misheard. I'm sure everything will be revealed in the coming weeks."

She heaved a contented sigh. "It makes you realize how fortunate we are to be free of people like that now."

219

It was after eleven when Ben and Martine stole downstairs and out into the darkness. Martine blew her silent whistle and the white giraffe came trotting over to the game park gate. She hadn't wanted to upset her grandmother on her first day back by asking if she could go for a Christmas Eve night ride on Jemmy, but she'd thought of the perfect compromise: Jemmy could come into the garden.

It wouldn't please Sampson, who tended the lawn and flowers, but it would keep her and Ben out of the jaws of any passing lions or snakes. After the week they'd just had, that had to be a positive thing.

Jemmy had no complaints about being led into Gwyn Thomas's neatly tended yard, especially since Martine and Ben lay down on the grass beneath the delicious honey-suckle tree. He wrapped his long tongue around the bell-like flowers and savored their nectar and the company of his human friends.

Martine felt the same joy at being close to her beloved white giraffe, who'd now be hers for years to come and not at the mercy of people who wanted to experiment on him or sell him to the highest bidder. And she was glad, as always, to be with her best friend. A lot of the healing and happiness she'd experienced this year was directly due to Ben's kindness, loyalty, and unwavering courage. It was comforting to know their destiny was interwoven.

"What are you thinking?" asked Ben, propping himself up on one elbow. His tousled black hair fell across his face.

A year ago, when Martine met him, he'd been the runt of Caracal School, as thin and small as she was, but since then he'd shot up and his muscles had filled out. He was, thought Martine, quite handsome.

"I'm thinking about how far we've come. On New Year's Eve I'll be twelve years old, and soon after that we'll be starting high school."

"High school! That's a scary thought," said Ben. "But it's exciting too. It'll be a new chapter with new adventures. Martine, do you really believe our destiny is going to be the one you saw in the cave pictures? That we'll be going around the world saving whales and polar bears and other endangered animals? That's quite a responsibility."

"It is," agreed Martine, "but we can do anything if we face it together."

Ben smiled at her. "I wouldn't want it any other way."

They lay there in silence for a while, listening to the sounds of Sawubona's night creatures and breathing in the sweet fragrance of the frangipani and mango trees. Above them, the white giraffe was outlined like a silver statue against the night sky, his head quite literally in the stars.

Ben checked his watch. "Hey, Martine, it's one minute past midnight. It's Christmas morning! We made it. Against all the odds, we made it."

Martine laughed. She jumped up and gave the white giraffe a Christmas kiss and he lowered his head to nuzzle her back. "Yes, we did, but Jemmy, we couldn't have done it without you." ❧

Author's Note

One of my clearest childhood memories is going to a farm close to ours in Africa to see fifty baby elephants. They'd been orphaned in a cull and were on their way to zoos across the world. I'm not a fan of zoos and wasn't then, and I'm dead set against culling—the practice of killing elephants "for their own good" if there are too many in a particular area. But, though I feared for the future of the babies, I was entranced by them. I sat on the corral fence and watched them tussle and play and rush around their enclosure on ungainly legs, little trunks swinging, and thought they were beyond adorable.

Over the years I've been fortunate enough to have many opportunities to be around elephants. I've rubbed their rough, prickly hides, cooed over their long eyelashes, watched them wallow joyously in muddy water holes, ridden them, and been charged by them in safari vehicles. But like Martine in *The Elephant's Tale,* I'd never really given much thought to the intelligence and astonishing natural gifts of elephants until I discovered how their acute hearing means they are able to pick up communications from other elephants from as far as six miles away. Or that their family bonds are so strong that youngsters orphaned by culls wake up screaming with nightmares. Then I remembered the babies I'd seen on that farm and felt devastated.

On a more positive note, while I was writing *The Elephant's Tale* I was able to spend months researching elephant behavior. What I learned convinced me that we have to do everything in our power to save these magnificent creatures, with their intricate and loving communities. We can't do that unless, like Martine, we learn to understand them.

Another part of my research was traveling to Namibia, the setting for this story. It is one of the most breathtakingly beautiful countries in Africa, but its existence depends on a limited source of rainfall, which is increasingly being affected by global warming. Other desert regions, such as the Australian Outback, are in the same position. My own father, a farmer in the Southern African country of Zimbabwe, often tells me of the catastrophic changes in climate that he has witnessed in his lifetime. We're now using the resources of 1.4 earths. When those resources are gone, there'll be none left.

The best part about writing the *Legend of the Animal Healer* series has been living with characters whose mission is not only to heal and save animals but to make their lives better. There are nearly 6.8 billion people on earth. Imagine if every one of us did one small thing to help wildlife or the environment, the earth would soon begin to recover and we'd all benefit by having a more beautiful planet to enjoy.

The wonderful thing about the world now is that it has become a much smaller place. We're all connected. Don't ever feel that you're too far away to make a difference. The smallest action, whether it's stopping to be kind to a dog or cat on your way to school, or not dropping litter, or perhaps doing a school project on the endangered species of Africa, makes a difference, although you might not realize it at the time.

In the meantime, follow your dreams, follow your heart, and consider conservation.

Lauren St John,
London 2009

Acknowledgments

I've loved writing this series, but it would not have been possible without the faith and wisdom of my Orion editor, Fiona Kennedy; my agent, Catherine Clarke; and my Dial editor, Liz Waniewski. One of the best things about writing the books has been having Jon Foster, Antonio Javier Caparo, and David Dean bring them to life with their stunning illustrations. I'm immensely grateful to everyone else at Orion and Penguin for their support, hard work, and passionate commitment to children's publishing, especially Alexandra Nicholas, Helen Speedy, Sally Wray, Kate Christer, Jessica, Killingley, Pandora White, Victoria Nicholl, and Lisa Milton.

A special thank you to Ruth Wilson for doing me the huge honor of reading the audio books of *The White Giraffe* and *Dolphin Song*. Andjoa Andoh also did a fantastic job on the unabridged audio books. Last but definitely not least, thanks to Kellie Santin, for the faith and support, to my mum for her elephant research, to my dad for the Matopos road trip, and my sister, Lisa, for the Namibian adventure. Can't wait for the next one!